GW00480676

Inside the Orchestra

INSIDE THE ORCHESTRA

The story of the instruments

THE GREAT COMPOSERS • THE FINEST PLAYERS • THE BEST RECORDINGS

Rob Ainsley • Introduction by Jeremy J. Beadle

First published in 1994 by

Future Books

a division of Future Publishing Limited
Beauford Court, 30 Monmouth Street, Bath BA1 2BW

Photography acknowledgements on page 120.

Designed by Kate Elkin

Edited by Charles Searson

A CIP catalogue record for this book is available from the British Library

Isbn: 1 85981 0101

Printed and bound by BPC, Paulton Books Ltd.
A member of the British Printing Company

2 4 6 8 10 9 7 5 3 1

If you would like more information on our other classical music titles please write to: The Publisher, Future Books, at above address.

Contents

INSIDE THE ORCHESTRA

How the great orchestras have developed

'Orchestra' was originally a Greek word meaning 'a dancing place'. Sadly – and rather prosaically – this doesn't mean that orchestral players used to dance around while making music; it actually refers to the semicircular space at the front of the stage in a Greek theatre where the Chorus in a play would sing and dance.

It was in seventeenth-century France that the term was revived in a musical context, and a German book defined 'orchestra' as "a place in front of the stage where the instrumentalists and director sit." By the eighteenth century, the word transferred itself to the players. Before this time groups of instrumental players were usually known by the name of 'consorts' or even 'Chapels' (which is how some German conductors and orchestral directors became known as 'Kapellmeisters' or 'Chapel-masters').

It was the development of tuneful instruments which sounded pleasant playing together which first gave rise to purely instrumental ensembles. In the sixteenth century such groups would use just one instrument for each musical line; one of the crucial steps towards the orchestra as we know it came when musical ensembles started to 'double' string parts – that is, to have more than one violin or viola or cello playing a single musical line. When the first great opera, Monteverdi's *Orfeo*, was first performed at the court of Mantua in Italy in 1607, its use of strings 'doubled' in this way was a novelty.

Italian string consorts were established all over Europe during the sixteenth century, and it was from these that the first orchestras grew. King James I

increased the number of regular violin players in his permanent royal ensemble to ten in the early seventeenth century; even Monteverdi's orchestra for *Orfeo* had used only four! During the seventeenth century there was no established pattern to these embryonic orchestras; some included stringed instruments of all shapes and sizes, from violins to double-basses to plucked instruments like lutes and guitars; some (like the one used for *Orfeo*) employed wind and brass instruments – flutes, trumpets, cornets and trombones – even though these were still at a relatively primitive stage of their development. Often instruments would be specially introduced on a one-off basis for a certain effect; double-basses, for instance, would be used to impersonate thunder.

In the eighteenth century the orchestra as we know it began to take form. German and Austrian composers and musicians hit on a settled pattern for strings; reforms in wind instruments meant that oboes and flutes made a more reliable and tuneful noise. The German and Austrian model spread through most of Europe, and an 'orchestra' was defined by one writer as "an organised body of bowed strings with more than one player to each part, to which may be added any number of wind and percussion."

It's the predominance and numbers of string players that mark these early orchestras as the ancestors of today's big symphony orchestras. When Monteverdi's *Orfeo* was performed in 1607, there were no more violins than trumpets; when Handel's operas were performed in London in the 1720s, there

The modern orchestral layout as demonstrated by one of America's, and the world's, finest: the **Cleveland Orchestra.**

A Flutes
B Oboes
C Clarinets
D Bassoons
E French Horns
F Trumpets
G Trombones & Tuba
H Percussion
I Harp
J 1st Violins
K 2nd Violins
L Violas
M Cellos
N Double Basses

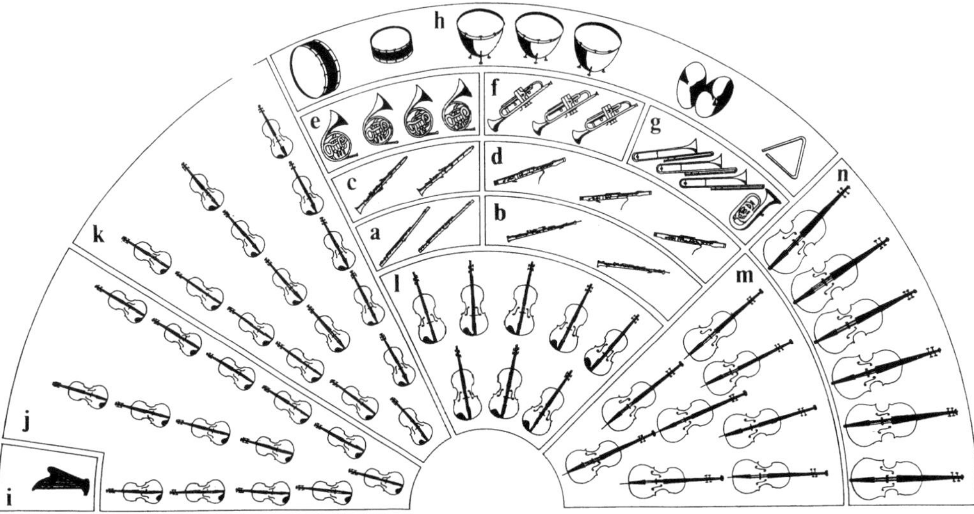

The **instruments** and section positions for a typical modern symphony orchestra.

were 22 violinists, with nine wind players in total (flutes, oboes, bassoons and horns). One of the most important eighteenth-century orchestras was established in the German town of Mannheim; by the 1770s it had become a model orchestra which influenced the way that Haydn and Mozart (among others) wrote for the orchestra. Its line-up included 20 violins, four violas, four cellos and four double-basses with three flutes, three oboes, three clarinets (some of the first 'regular' orchestral clarinets) and four bassoons, as well as four horns, two trumpets and a set of timpani and a keyboard from which the director would control the performance. The Mannheim orchestra was large by the standards of the time and allowed for certain musical effects not possible with smaller ensembles; one such was the famous 'Mannheim crescendo,' a dramatic increase in volume.

The size of orchestras at this time (and much of the time since) depended on finance. In the eighteenth century, orchestras tended to be court affairs, paid for by princes and noblemen at the various courts of Europe when the continent was much more divided into little duchies and principalities. Haydn, for example, ran an orchestra at the Austrian court of Prince Esterházy; it was, inevitably, a smaller affair than the one at Mannheim with only ten violins, no clarinets or trumpets or timpani and two of everything else. Sometimes these orchestras would find themselves out of a job if one patron died or was deposed to be replaced by someone who didn't care much about music. When composers weren't working for a specific patron and wanted to get orchestras together, they'd sometimes try and raise subscriptions in advance for a series of concerts to pay for an orchestra and somewhere to perform; this was the way Mozart went about things after he moved to Vienna in the 1780s. However, patronage was the more secure way for musicians to live, even if it did mean dependency upon whim and caprice. But a new element of confusion was introduced by the upheavals of the Napoleonic Wars.

Despite European politics, the orchestra continued to grow. The last half of the eighteenth century had witnessed the development of the symphony, which involved the orchestra playing together (usually) without singers or instrumental soloists. Originally a 'symphony' had just been the short introduction to an opera. But as patrons wanted to show off their orchestras, they required a musical form which wasn't a showcase for singers or for solo instrumentalists. Around the middle of the century, C P E Bach and Haydn started to produce these orchestral showcases, and as the orchestra developed and acquired new instruments, so this form, the symphony, began to grow. Mozart, with over 40 symphonies, and Haydn, with over 100, turned the symphony into a major orchestral form; Haydn ensured its continued spread across Europe, writing symphonies for orchestras and audiences in Paris and London.

So when Beethoven began composing in the 1790s it was natural that he should turn to the symphony. And he had big ideas, which meant expanding the size of both the symphony and the orchestra. Beethoven's larger works required larger forces; he also made the use of all woodwind and all brass and timpani a matter of course. At a Beethoven concert in 1814, there were 36 violins, 14 violas, 12 cellos and as many as 17 double-basses, as well as two of each woodwind and brass instrument then developed. These were unusually large forces, perhaps; the premiere of the great Ninth Symphony, the *Choral* – the largest symphonic work yet written – used 24 violins, and scaled the other strings down accordingly. But the size of orchestra demanded by Beethoven's music came to be accepted as standard, and it was these kind of forces which composers like Berlioz, Schubert, Schumann and Mendelssohn had in mind. Indeed, Mendelssohn wanted a deeper brass sound, and experimented with now obsolete instruments like the ophicleide and the serpent, which were superseded by the invention of the bass tuba in the 1830s.

During the nineteenth century, the technology of musical instruments was refined to make them more like those we're used to today. Stringed instruments became capable of making more noise, going further up the scale and making a generally smoother sound; trumpets, horns and trombones had valves added, which made them also sound smoother and more reliable at keeping pitch. Orchestral composers could now go in for bigger and better dramatic effects. New standards of professionalism appeared, too, and the first orchestras in the entirely modern sense were founded; self-governing groups of musicians based in one place, often developing a distinctive style of playing. The most famous of all orchestras (arguably), the Vienna Philharmonic, was founded in 1842; and both the Liverpool and New York Philharmonics can trace their origins back to the same decade. Of course, different orchestras evolved different local traditions and styles, often arising from the music which they played most regularly; and these styles and reputations continue to distinguish the best orchestras. For instance, the Vienna Philharmonic has its own glorious string sound, with a lively sense of rhythm, as anyone who's ever heard one of their New Year Strauss concerts can testify; while the Czech Philharmonic has a slightly earthier sound, with a distinctive woodwind timbre, especially suitable for playing Eastern European composers like Dvorak. Some orchestras have developed a reputation as technicians; both the Berlin Philharmonic and the Chicago Symphony Orchestra are proficient in a vast range of different music, with impressive brass sections and a solid, awesome sound when playing all together.

As orchestras grew larger, the role of the conductor became increasingly important. Originally conductors had simply kept time, actually doing so by thumping a long stick on the ground (it was in this way that the composer Lully managed to stab himself in the foot, dying from the resultant gangrene). In the eighteenth century, direction usually came from a keyboard; musical directors would play a bass-line and dictate the music's rhythm. However, the larger works of the nineteenth century and the larger forces involved demanded a firmer controlling hand. It was, perhaps, the music of Richard Wagner, which helped to create the cult of the conductor; Wagner himself, his friend Hans Richter, and then composers like Richard Strauss and Mahler, all furthered the idea of the professional conductor who didn't just keep time, but became the focal point of the orchestra, shaping the interpretation and directing the musicians so as to put across his personal view of the music.

Wagner's music not only began the cult of the conductor; it led to a quantum leap in the way that composers regarded the orchestra. When the *Ring* cycle was performed in the 1870s, the string section alone numbered 64 (almost twice the size of the entire orchestra used in *Orfeo*), and the sound created by large wind and brass sections (including eight horns) gave the composers of the next generation – Richard Strauss, Mahler and Schoenberg – new ideas and ambitions. Mahler's Eighth (1910) became known as the "Symphony of a Thousand" as it was reckoned that it needed that number of participants. Strauss's opera *Elektra* (1908) and Schoenberg's choral work *Gurrelieder* (1911) both demanded orchestras which were large even by the standards of the day; among other things, *Gurrelieder* requires eight flutes, ten horns and seven trombones, a far cry from the symphonies of Haydn and Mozart.

As the orchestra became more diverse and capable of more intricate sound, composers became interested in writing works which explored the sonorities now possible. Tchaikovsky's ballet music – especially *The Nutcracker* (1892) – does this, even, in the "Dance of the Sugar Plum Fairy", introducing the sound of a new keyboard instrument, the celesta. Richard Strauss, in tone poems like *Don Quixote* (1897), used different instruments to play different characters, with a splendid wind cacophony portraying a flock of sheep. This is also how a famous piece like Prokofiev's *Peter and the Wolf* (1936) works; while other composers were fascinated just to see what intensities of sound they could get out of the orchestra. This is the motivating force of the mad, persistent rhythms of Ravel's famous *Boléro* (1928), designed as an exercise in orchestration; on a more extended level, Bartók wrote a *Concerto for Orchestra* (1943), in which all the different instrumental sections are allowed their share of the limelight, especially in a series of wind duets which make up a movement called "Giuoco delle Copie" ("Game of Pairs").

After the First World War, there was a reaction against the size of the 'established' orchestra. Modern composers such as Schoenberg and Stravinsky, despite their own talents for writing for huge orchestras, favoured a return to more classical ensembles; and the economic situation certainly made it harder

Gerard Dépardieu, playing Marin Marais in the film "Tous les Matins du monde", showing how baroque conductors banged a staff on the floor to keep time.

to support huge musical groups. Nevertheless, certain orchestras were, by this time, vital and integral parts of the musical scene; the Vienna Philharmonic, the Berlin Philharmonic, the Czech Philharmonic and the Dutch Concertgebouw on the continent of Europe, the Liverpool Philharmonic and the London Symphony Orchestra in Britain, the Boston and Chicago Symphony Orchestras in the United States. Although there were no patrons in the old sense, new patronage sprang from the broadcasting corporations, giving us such now distinguished ensembles as the BBC Symphony Orchestra and the RSO Berlin.

Arturo Toscanini, one of this century's most famous conductors, fixed the image of the conductor in popular imagination: outspoken, dictatorial, brilliant.

Record companies, too, would create orchestras for famous conductors like Arturo Toscanini and Otto Klemperer. But the survival of orchestras has become more and more a matter of economics. While there will never be any serious threat to the most famous orchestras, others rely on the personalities of their musical directors and try to balance established favourites and new music to cater for all audiences.

However, there's no reason to get too gloomy about the orchestra's future; many modern composers seem to have returned to the idea of writing music aimed at the traditional large Symphony orchestra. After all, there is no substitute for one of the world's great orchestras going at full tilt.

TOP ORCHESTRAS

Vienna Philharmonic Orchestra

Arguably the most impressive orchestra in the world, distinguished by its gloriously smooth string sound, equipped with a good sense of rhythm and equally at home in the romping world of Johann Strauss or the sardonic, bitter-sweet Mahler.

Berlin Philharmonic Orchestra

Still bears the imprint of its long-time conductor Herbert von Karajan; extraordinary power and force, and probably the most muscular orchestra around. The BPO has always sounded especially good in Beethoven, Bruckner and Richard Strauss.

Chicago Symphony Orchestra

The Chicago Symphony makes a formidably impressive noise with especially well-honed brass. It's attracted modern commissions which always make sure that brass section is well catered for, and is equally at home in Tchaikovsky and Stravinsky.

Royal Concertgebouw Orchestra

Holland's leading orchestra has an astonishing versatility, sounding solid with a touch of gypsy in Brahms, witty and sharp in Mozart and Schubert, and marvellous with Mahler. The Concertgebouw responds equally well to conductors with markedly different styles.

London Symphony Orchestra

Choosing between several fine British orchestras is difficult, but the LSO has always attracted big-name conductors and shown versatility through the whole classical repertoire; a subtle power-house, with a good sense of rhythm.

Montreal Symphony Orchestra

Under conductor Charles Dutoit, this Canadian band has turned into a great recording orchestra, with superb instrumental colour and a real flair for early-twentieth-century music.

TOP CDs

To hear the Vienna Philharmonic at play – yet entirely serious and committed – their New Year's Day Concert under Carlos Kleiber (the best of their modern conductors) is hugely enjoyable (Sony CD48376). Their power in great symphonies is well displayed in a live 1987 performance of Mahler's Fifth, under the inspirational guidance of Leonard Bernstein (Deutsche Grammophon 431 037-2).

One of the best Berlin Philharmonic recordings in recent years is their Bruckner Ninth Symphony with Daniel Barenboim (Teldec 9031-72140-2); while the versatility of the Concertgebouw is reflected by a 1970s version of Brahms's Violin Concerto (Philips 422 972-2) and their 1990s award-winning Schubert Symphonies (Teldec 4509-91184-2).

Some of the best 'orchestral showcase' music has been superbly recorded by the Montreal Symphony Orchestra. Their version of Bartók's *Concerto for Orchestra* is dazzling (Decca 421 443-2), while any of their Ravel performances are to be commended; *Boléro* comes with the seductive *Rapsodie espagnole* and another maniacal orchestral showpiece, *La Valse* (Decca 410 010-2).

Jeremy J. Beadle
London, 1994

THE VIOLIN

The "most perfect instrument" of the orchestra

The history of the violin is a succession of great players and great works spanning the whole development of Western music. Since it first sprang fully formed from Northern Italy during the 1500s, the instrument has undergone few changes; it hasn't needed them. The size and string tension is ideal for the hand, giving maximum potential for technical facility; on the viola for example, which is only slightly longer, violin-style pyrotechnics are virtually impossible. The bow gives the facility for rapidly repeated notes or sustained notes of any length, giving tremendous variety of expressive effects. And the sound quality can be exploited by sensitive players to give the same penetrating range of emotion as the human voice: it is an instrument "built for singing", as one player put it. So composers and players have been able for hundreds of years to concentrate on the music, unfettered by instrumental limitations, making the violin one of the most stable currencies of musical thought.

In the fourteenth and fifteenth centuries the country fiddler playing jigs and dances was already a familiar part of village life. But as organised music-making developed during and after the Renaissance, the versatile violin became an essential part of the orchestra, and composers like Monteverdi started using it prominently in the orchestra in the seventeenth century. Up till then the main instrumental family had been the viols, string instruments superficially similar to violins but unrelated in construction; but the bright tone of the violin and its potential for fast, accurate playing better suited the new music written in the early baroque period. In 1700 Archangelo Corelli wrote six "Church Sonatas" and six "Chamber Sonatas" for violin and small orchestra. This Op. 5 set was an important summarisation of the styles of the previous century and was played all over Europe. In the next few years, the distinction between "church" and "chamber" music styles disappeared.

Many violinist-composers such as Vivaldi, Tartini and Locatelli were writing increasingly complex violin music. Vivaldi's *Four Seasons* – actually part of a set of 12 violin concertos called *The Trial Between Harmony and Invention* – were just as popular immediately after they were written in 1725 as they are today, though they fell into disuse between Vivaldi's death in 1741 and their revival as 'lift music' a few decades ago. Vivaldi himself was a gifted violinist who often stunned audiences by playing "impossible" music, and found the time to compose around 220 other violin concertos, many of them showing off his innovative harmonic and technical side.

Solo violin music had come a long way from rural dance tunes, and by the late 1600s composers such as Biber had been writing extended solo pieces for the instrument. J S Bach's six Sonatas and Partitas for violin, written in 1720, remain at one of the cornerstones of the solo repertoire, unsurpassed either in technical or artistic use of the instrument. The set is epic in scale, filling two CDs. They present supreme interpretational and technical difficulties: at some points not only double-stopping (playing two notes at the same time) is called for, but also treble- and even quadruple-stopping, which would use all four strings at the same time. Bach must have had a sequential, rather than simultaneous, effect in mind. This didn't

Paganini's body was refused burial on sacred ground because it was rumoured that his talent had come from an unholy business deal.

stop one twentieth-century Danish maker from designing a special 'Bach bow' which could be relaxed by the player flicking a switch, so that the slackened hairs would fit around all four strings and thus play the multiple stoppings exactly as written. There is a formidable amount of music in the set: each partita or sonata is made up of several pieces, and the Second Partita ends with the famous Chaconne, nearly 15 minutes long just by itself, and substantial enough a piece of music to have been arranged as a piano piece by both Brahms and Busoni.

Violin technique was developing rapidly as the music demanded more of the player. Leopold Mozart, an Austrian violinist and composer, became a household name in European music circles after publishing an influential book on violin technique in 1756 (the year that saw the birth of his son Wolfgang, who was to become quite a famous composer himself). The book, *Versuch einer gründlichen Violinschule*, is an important guide for modern performers who wish to play music of that period in a style authentic to that period (it advises against overdoing vibrato, for example, one of the shibboleths of authentic playing).

Mozart junior – thanks to pressure from his father – played the violin to professional standard from an early age and wrote around 26 sonatas (violin plus keyboard) and five concertos, of which the last three have become standard concert items. (Any with numbers bigger than five are not by Mozart!) The most popular is the fifth, with its haunting slow introduction to the first movement, the beautiful *Adagio*, and elaborate Minuetto with the "alla turca" ("Turkish-style") section which gave it the nickname the Turkish. And all written by a 19 year old!

Mozart's works were an inspiration for the young Beethoven and Schubert, fellow members of the "Viennese School". Beethoven, though a gifted pianist like Mozart, was not a good violinist: his playing was described as "dreadful" by his student Ries. But his violin writing took up where Mozart left off, increasing the technical demands on the player and, in his sonatas, stressing the partnership and interplay between the keyboard player and soloist. And Beethoven's Violin Concerto broke significant new ground.

As with many such works, though, Beethoven's Violin Concerto was not understood until well after his death. The premiere was given in 1806 by Franz Clement; between movements, Clement gave some light relief with a few violin tricks which included picking out melodies on one string and playing with the instrument upside down! But Beethoven's original approach to the concerto, which was more of a symphony than an opportunity to display virtuosity, didn't impress the crowds, and the work was played just four times in the next 38 years. It was only when Joseph Joachim, a young Hungarian violinist who rapidly became the great concerto player of his century, 'revived' the work in a performance conducted by Mendelssohn in 1844 that it became established.

Now, of course, it is one of the essentials of the repertoire, though it has continued to attract controversy. The cadenza in a concerto – the opportunity for the soloist to play a flashy and improvised section unaccompanied – had by the 1800s lost its improvisatory nature and become a prepared piece. The 'improvisation' that Joachim prepared is only one of many that have been written. The modern Russian composer Alfred Schnittke has written one which, bewilderingly for some purists, quotes the 'hook' lines of other violin concertos by Mendelssohn and Brahms among others – which weren't written for many decades after Beethoven's death. But perhaps the joke is meant to be on the purists: the flashy, tongue-in-cheek nature of the Schnittke cadenza is probably more in keeping with the spirit of Clement's bizarre first performance.

After Beethoven's masterpiece, the big romantic violin concerto became a favourite form of concert-goers and composers. The 15 concertos of Louis Spohr are often thought of as being a bridge between those of Beethoven and Mendelssohn, whose Concerto took six years to write (ending in 1844). With its technical ingenuity, romantic brilliance (and many innovatory structural ideas, such as the bridge between the *Andante* and finale, and the tying together of the first two movements) the Mendelssohn Concerto, premiered by Ferdinand David, became one of the best-known classical pieces ever written.

Joachim must have had a pretty impressive CV. In addition to the Mendelssohn Concerto, he had major works written for him by Dvorak, Bruch, Brahms and Schumann, premiering many such works which have since become part of the music listener's staple diet. The warm Bruch Concerto No. 1 (he wrote three) has become almost as popular as the Mendelssohn, probably due to the fact that it is almost obligatorily coupled with it on recordings; the Schumann work – written when his mental health was deteriorating and his mind was growing tired – was a disappointment. Joachim kept on to the manuscript, refusing to publish it for fear of tarnishing the great man's reputation after his death.

There were no such problems with the Brahms Concerto. Joachim and Brahms corresponded during its composition and after its premiere in 1879, and Joachim advised the composer over some technical impossibilities in the piece. Brahms only took part of the violinist's advice, with the result that the work is ferociously difficult to play, though for sound musical reasons rather than ignorance on Brahms's part. Musically the work followed Beethoven's symphonic model, and is considered by some as the definitive Violin Concerto.

Tchaikovsky's Violin Concerto, written in 1878, is another difficult and popular work, but for sheer technical virtuosity, the solo caprices written by Nicolò Paganini in the early part of the nineteenth century remain some of the most testing pieces ever attempted. Paganini's playing technique was so astounding that it is said his body was refused burial in Nice on consecrated ground because of rumours that his powers had come from an unholy business deal. He was possibly the fastest and most virtuosic violinist that has ever lived: playing his *Movemento Perpetuo* he clocked in at 3:03 – a rate of over 12 notes per second, cited by the *Guinness Book of Music* as the fastest violin playing ever recorded.

Paganini used many innovatory techniques in his playing and composition, such as use of harmonics and left-hand pizzicatos (plucking of the string), but it was another violinist-composer, Ernst, who was regarded by Joachim and others as the greatest of their generation. His Concerto is in some ways more difficult than Paganini, and his *Variations on the Last Rose of Summer* requires a left hand pizzicato line at the same time as a conventional melodic line, also

Besides being a composer, **Vivaldi** was a gifted violinist who often stunned audiences by playing "impossible" music.

played with the left hand.

The twentieth century has seen plenty of violin concertos joining the already great repertoire, and virtually every major composer has been inspired to write in the genre: Sibelius, Glazunov, Reger, Elgar, Bloch, Nielsen, Delius, Szymanowski, Schoenberg, Hindemith, Bartók, Walton, Britten, Berg, Stravinsky, Prokofiev, Khachaturian, Shostakovich… the list is endless, and often – because of the expressive nature of the violin – the works are very much bound up with the musical personality of the composers. Bartók's Second Concerto is recognised as one of the great masterpieces of the century, and has become a familiar part of the repertory despite its unusual technical problems and unfamiliar musical idiom. Shostakovich's First Concerto, written for David Oistrakh, lay completed but hidden in a drawer between 1948 and 1955 because it would have been dangerous for the composer to release such a brooding work in a political climate that demanded optimistic pro-Communist songs. Elgar's Concerto dreams poignantly for a lost world that possibly didn't exist outside the imagination; Ravel's sonatas for violin are often bluesy in character; Berg's Concerto, despite being laughed at after its first performance for its unlistenably difficult idiom, has been established as a modern masterpiece, regarded now as warm and appealing. Schoenberg said his Concerto required six fingers to play; Khachaturian's underrated Concerto is a strong and irresistible piece, inspired by Armenian musical impulses; Walton's Concerto is lyrical and bittersweet, and was written for Jascha Heifetz who found it too easy and asked the composer to write a more challenging fast movement.

And so it goes on. The composer wishing to write a concerto now has the disadvantage that it seems impossible to say something that hasn't already been said in the huge solo and symphonic literature of the violin; yet such is the versatility and expressive range of the violin that there is always something new to find.

So violin players, particularly compared to other soloists, are unimaginably well-off in terms of repertoire. But if they want to play the masterworks on a master violin, such as a Stradivarius or a Guarneri, they need to be unimaginably well-off in terms of money too. A 1720 Strad named the Mendelssohn was bought on behalf of an anonymous player at

Christie's in 1990 for £902,000 – the highest price ever publicly paid for an instrument. It is reckoned that some violins would fetch well over £1 million if they ever come onto the open market.

The craftsmanship and technique needed to assemble the 70-odd parts of a violin have not really been bettered since the golden period between 1650 and 1750, when makers such as Antonio Stradivari (1644–1737, known as Stradivarius) Giuseppe Guarneri (1666–1740) Nicolò Amati (1596-1684) and their families were all active in Cremona. Strads, Guarneris, Amatis and the like are certainly the best money can buy: players talk lovingly of the beautiful character and colour of the sound, the evenness through the range, and the ease of playing: the music carries to the back of the hall with less effort. But the prices have become inflated because such violins are treated as *objets d'art* rather than working tools, and have become commodities bought and sold by investors.

The **Mendelssohn Stradivarius** of 1720 fetched the unsurpassed figure of £902,000 at Christies in 1990.

Many makers have tried to emulate the conditions in which Stradivarius worked to produce violins like his. One maker in America used wood stored underwater to make the body – as he believes Stradivarius did in waterlogged Venice – and employed resin containing crushed amber. But perhaps the reason why Stradivarius produced so many outstanding-quality violins is simpler. As Andreas Woywod, a violin maker and restorer at Biddulph's in London, points out, Stradivari had a very long working life: he was still making instruments when he died aged 94, having started 80 years earlier. So, with all the expertise he gained, there were almost bound to be some extraordinary examples out of the thousands of violins he must have made. Modern instruments are made in virtually the same way and with the same materials – but because wood is a natural substance, tiny variations in the grain and substance can make significant differences to the result – even two violins made from the same tree will sound slightly different.

Indeed, many modern violins come out very well in tests compared to their predecessors that cost up to a hundred times the price, and players talk of the recent renaissance in British violin making.

There have been a few changes to the violin over the years. As concert halls grew in size in the mid 1800s, string instruments needed to be brighter and project better, so the string tension was increased by tilting the fingerboard down. Gut strings were in use until 1700, when the G string was usually wound with wire to brighten the tone, and this century steel strings have become the norm.

But the differences bet-ween old and new instruments aren't really that great; the old Strads and Guarneris can be changed to the new shape with only minor modifications, and the player who wishes to play pre-1830 music in the authentic way has to adjust their playing style, rather than their technique.

There have been many outstanding violinists since Joachim opened up the repertoire in the last century. The "golden age" of playing between the 1930s and 1950s saw artists such as (in no particular order) Heifetz, Oistrakh, Szering, Ricci, Menuhin, Stern, Francescatti, Elman, Milstein, and Grumiaux. The traditional Russo-Jewish influence in violin playing has since been enriched by a variety of artists from other parts of the world. Clearly non-Semitic names such as Xue-Wei (from China) Kyung-Wha Chung (Korea) and Midori (Japan) are familiar to modern listeners. Chung and Midori, along with Lydia Mordkovitch, Anne-Sophie Mutter and Viktoria Mullova are continuing the female tradition of violinists set by virtuosos such as Jelly d'Aranyi, Ginette Neveu, Marie Hall and Ida Haendel.

Such is the breadth of the violin that it has even embraced "pop star" figures such as Nigel Kennedy in Britain and Joshua Bell in the US. Bell was promoted as the artist in the "world's first classical music pop video", playing Brahms's *Hungarian Rhapsody* No. 2, and Kennedy became a familiar figure in Britain through TV appearances ranging from performances of the Berg Violin Concerto to airing his football views on sports programmes. Though many music listeners disapproved of his affected post-punk appearance and contrived sarf-landan accent, the general opinion among violin players of all ages was that the quality of his playing saved the situation from being distasteful hype; and if he could kindle excitement for the classics in a popular audience, even through a bit of media mischief, then so much the better. He gave up full-time classical playing and recording in 1992 to concentrate on personal projects in other musical areas, but we hope he will be making more recordings.

If there is a downside to the tremendous popularity of the instrument it is that young players find themselves under increasing pressure at an early age. Teenage prodigies such as Maxim Vengerov (born 1974) and Sarah Chang (who was born in 1981 and recorded her first CD when she was nine) are nowadays being produced with the sort of intense training more often associated with Olympic athletes, and there is the danger that such premature pressure will have a detrimental effect on the artistic side of the player.

After all, the violin is arguably the most expressive instrument, with a direct line to the heart as well as the head; a player needs in their personality the mixture of theory and experience of life, of the intellectual and the gypsy, to do what violin music does perhaps better than any other instrument: to express the ineffable.

THE FINEST PERFORMERS

Selected by Samuel Fischer, a violin teacher and former recitalist

No doubt who's top of the list: Jascha Heifetz, the Russian-born American violinist. Quite simply he was the best – and still would be. The clarity of his playing even in the fastest passages, his subtle fingerings and ability to appeal to the heart remain unsurpassed even today: he was many decades ahead of his time. Fritz Kreisler of Austria was another great player of the older generation who practised even less than Heifetz. His sweet tone and rich vibrato were unmatched at the time.

The Russian David Oistrakh was one of the other great players in the "golden age" of the 1930s to the 1950s. His technical mastery and lack of affectation has made some criticise him for being "anonymous"; in fact, he was simply concentrating on the message in the music, which is usually just what is required.

Pinchas Zukerman and Itzhak Perlman, both from

Nigel Kennedy became a familiar figure in Britain through TV appearances ranging from performances of the Berg Violin Concerto to airing his views on football.

Israel, show the strong and emotional Jewish character of the violin, and Perlman, who took up the violin at the age of four after losing the use of his legs through polio, in particular often has the touch of the gypsy about him; Zukerman's playing of the Elgar Concerto, and Perlman's of the Beethoven Concerto, are both excellent.

Gidon Kremer of Latvia is worth picking out too – the "thinking man's Nigel Kennedy" if you like. A player with a fine intellectual grasp of his music, he nevertheless has no qualms about playing the unusual – such as Schnittke's cadenza to the Beethoven Concerto that quotes from several other violin concertos that were written after Beethoven's!

To the list must be added Yehudi Menuhin, not only as the neckmark against which young prodigies are judged (the combination of distinctive virtuosity with his amazing, unique tone, the ability to hold an audience not by fireworks but by integrity, spiritual and interpretative insight, and his timing, all in his early teens) but also as a "world musician" who has worked with Indian and other types of music, and someone who has made great initiatives in teaching: the Menuhin School in Surrey provides a well-balanced, all-round education for young violin virtuosos – football and fun as well as lots of music practice and performance!

A name to watch for is among a number of excellent young players is the extraordinarily talented Russian teenager Maxim Vengerov.

And this hasn't mentioned Nathan Milstein, Arthur Grumiaux, Misha Elman, Kyung-Wha Chung, Anne-Sophie Mutter, Monica Huggett, Ruggiero Ricci, Isaac Stern... the list goes on and on.

The Best CD Recordings

Chosen by Samuel Fischer

The definitive violin recording is Jascha Heifetz playing Bruch's *Scottish Fantasy*. In virtually one take, he makes otherwise ordinary music sound vibrant, energetic and exciting, with warmth and clarity even in the fastest sections, and superb subtlety of fingering and colour. Simple music which speaks direct to the heart (RCA RD 86214).

Yehudi Menuhin's playing of the Elgar Violin Concerto as a 16 year old has many parallels with Jacqueline Du Pré's playing of his Cello Concerto. There's a strange mixture of strength and frail beauty that seems to remind us of our own mortality. Menuhin plays with living rubato based on impulse, with apparent abandon yet complete control of sound, and a warm vocal style (EMI CDH7 69786-2).

The Berg Violin Concerto is an essential part of the modern repertoire, even though people laughed at its first performance. It isn't easy listening, but Itzhak Perlman's heartfelt, "gypsy" playing makes it very amenable (Deutsche Grammophon 413 725-2).

The Bach Sonatas and Partitas are the biggest challenge to any player and there's no such thing as the perfect performance; but Sigiswald Kuijken's CD of the

Yehudi Menuhin is possessed with the combination of distinctive virtuosity, unique tone, and the ability to hold an audience not by fireworks, but by artistic integrity.

set brings out the imagination, joy, gravity, humour (such as in the E major Gavotte) and the almost macho architectural power of the three big fugues (Deutsche Harmonia Mundi GD77043).

An interesting insight onto a familiar piece comes from Leonid Kavakos's playing of the Sibelius Violin Concerto in its original 1904 form, before the composer made some fairly major revisions and came up with the version we know today (BIS CD500).

Essential masterpieces on CD to go for include Chung's Second Bartók Concerto with Solti on Decca 425 015-2; the Nielsen Concerto with Cho-Liang Lin and Swedish Radio (Sony CD44548); Xue-Wei's recording of Strauss's early Concerto and a new work by Christopher Headington on ASV CDDCA780; and Lydia Mordkovitch's fine Shostakovich Concertos with the Scottish National Orchestra under Neeme Järvi on Chandos CHAN8820.

One of my favourite authentic violin recordings is Vivaldi's *Four Seasons* played by Simon Standage, probably the best thing he's done. It's a real shaft of new light and a challenge to the old recordings (Archiv 400 045-2).

Finally a mention of the great worth of historic recordings which have been reissued on CD. Biddulph deserves a special mention: despite the surface noise of the early recordings, the artistry of players such as a very young Menuhin shines through. Then there's Heifetz playing the first recordings of concertos by Sibelius, Glazunov, and Prokofiev No. 2 (RCA RD87019); Louis Krasner playing the Berg Concerto conducted by the composer on Testament SBT1004; and Szigeti in the Bartók Rhapsody No. 1 with the composer on the piano (Biddulph LAB070/1).

THE VIOLA
More than just a big violin...

Two violins, one viola and one cello make a string quartet – and clearly show the difference in size of the members of the string family.

The quickest way to annoy a viola player is to call their instrument a "big violin". As they will quickly point out, the word violin actually means "little viola" (and cello is short for violoncello which means "little big viola"). It's not the etymology they're worried about, but the fact that the viola tends to dismissed as a mutant violin, and not regarded as an instrument with its own playing techniques, traditions and repertoire – despite the fact that it has been around in its present form for over 300 years.

Superficially the similarities are more obvious than the differences. Both instruments have four strings tuned a fifth apart, both are made in the same way, and the techniques of playing are close enough for a skilful player of either one to play the other. On the face of it the viola does indeed seem to be a violin made one-quarter bigger but the implications of the size difference run to more subtle things.

First, the larger fingerboard means longer stretches for the fingers, and less agility. Second, the longer strings mean a darker, less delicate sound, especially in the lower regions. Third, a viola bow has to be shorter and heavier than that of a violin in order to coax a sound out of the larger strings, making bow control more difficult. The consequence is that viola music is not just violin music transposed down a fifth and written in the alto clef instead of the treble. It has to concentrate much less on the athletics and much more on the dark expressive power of the instrument, as does the player.

The Viola and Violin Concertos of William Walton, written in the 1920s and 1930s respectively, show the differences up sharply. The Violin Concerto is full of bittersweet melodies and astonishing virtuoso pyrotechnics (in fact, its dedicatee, Jascha Heifetz, thought the first draft too easy and asked Walton to make the second movement more challenging); the Viola Concerto on the other hand is dark and sombre, with deeper and more penetrating lines. Even Bach, whose music is supposedly the 'purest' of all composers (in that the same piece can be played on almost any instrument) wrote differently for the viola and violin. One of the *Brandenburg Concertos*, unusually for the eighteenth century, features solo violas.

This hasn't stopped violin players dabbling with viola music. Nigel Kennedy, for example, has recorded both Walton concertos on the same disc; Pinchas Zukerman and Yehudi Menuhin are two others who have tried the switch. But all too often it just doesn't work. A violin player on the viola may hit all the right notes, but the sound is rarely right; it's too bright, too nonchalant, and the bottom strings lose their velvety tone.

It takes a genuine viola virtuoso to get the best out of viola music – the only problem has been finding them. Until the twentieth century the image of viola players was that they were generally second-rate violin players, and even now there are few genuine violists around. The viola was a mere makeweight in the orchestra, there to bulk out the sound between the cellos and violins; often the viola lines merely duplicate those of the others, or plod along supplying background rhythmic or melodic accompaniment. Considering the thousands of works produced by Telemann and Bach in the 1700s, the handful of viola works they wrote (a viola concerto and handful of chamber pieces by Telemann, and the *Brandenburg* No. 6 by Bach) shows there was evidently little call for viola music. Even in Mozart's rich and inspired creations, you find a lot of violists complaining that they get to play the duller parts.

In fact, if it hadn't been for Haydn, the instrument may have died out altogether. He established a new form of music in the 1760s: the string quartet, with two violins, a cello, and a viola. He wrote getting on for a hundred of them, so there must have been a demand. His quartets have always been overshadowed by his hundred-plus symphonies, but by providing a stock of excellent music he kept viola playing as a living art in the late 1700s. Beethoven's string quartets of the early nineteenth century include some very difficult parts for viola, so there must have been some skilful players around, but there was still no virtuoso music for them to play.

It seems that viola playing was in a Catch 22. Viola players were generally second rate, so there was no good music being written. And because there was no good viola music, talented string players chose the violin or cello.

Even a solid addition to the viola repertoire by Berlioz failed to stimulate the market. Paganini, possibly the most demonically talented violin virtuoso who ever lived, dabbled on the viola, and asked Berlioz to write a piece for the instrument in 1834. The result was *Harold in Italy*, a viola concerto, one of the few nineteenth-century viola works. Unfortunately Paganini didn't like the piece; it didn't have the flashy fingerwork he liked to show off when playing the violin (not, of course, that it should have done anyway) and had "too many rests".

Brahms wrote two sonatas for viola and piano, but these were actually arrangements of two clarinet sonatas. Consequently there are some phrases that don't quite work – wide leaps, for example, that are easy on a clarinet but which involve tricky cross-string jumps or ambitious glissandi on the viola. The nineteenth century was a time of few works and even fewer players who could play them.

The only way to break the vicious circle would be for a dedicated virtuoso player come through and, by sheer force of musical personality, establish the viola as a valid solo instrument. It fell to Englishman Lionel Tertis to rescue the instrument in the early part of the twentieth century.

Pinchas Zukerman is one of the handful of violin virtuosos who has also made a success of playing the viola.

One way he did this was to arrange a large amount of music for the viola. His transcription of Elgar's Cello Concerto, for example, is currently enjoying a revival with performances and recordings. Transcription can be a dangerous game to play; music can often seem thin and watered-down when played on a different instrument, out of context, and lukewarm concert programmes containing transcriptions can reinforce the idea that an instrument is dull and so not worth writing for. Tertis, however, managed to make his work. He brought the viola back in the public eye and in 1928 persuaded William Walton to write a concerto that was to re-establish the viola as a concert instrument.

Unfortunately Tertis wasn't keen on the result (Walton revised the work in 1961) and declined to premiere it, though he later played it a lot. The work was eventually premiered by Paul Hindemith, who in addition to composing a lot of music for the viola including several concertos and pieces for viola and small orchestra, was a fine viola player himself.

There followed something of a renaissance, with fine pieces coming from composers such as Vaughan Williams, Britten and Bartók. Britten's *Lachrymae,* based on a song of John Dowland, was written in 1950 for viola and piano but subsequently arranged for viola and orchestra. Bartók's Viola Concerto was his last piece, left incomplete on his death in 1945 and subsequently finished by Tibor Szerli. Bartók was in acute pain in the last stages of leukaemia as he wrote the work, and it shows in the music.

Another swan-song was the Viola Sonata of Dmitri Shostakovich, written a few weeks before his death in 1975, and regarded by many as one of the finest modern pieces for the instrument. It was first played by Fyodor Druzhinin and Mikhail Muntian in the composer's flat a few weeks after he died, and the last movement paraphrases Beethoven's *Moonlight* Sonata to give an air of great serenity. Maxim, the composer's son, says you can "feel your soul flying to heaven".

The viola in the 1990s looks set to become a more popular solo instrument again. A significant modern partnership has arisen between the increasingly familiar figure of the Russian player Yuri Bashmet and his compatriot Alfred Schnittke, who has written several important works including a Viola Concerto and his recent *Monologue* for viola and chamber orchestra. They are both good examples of late twentieth-century writing and, while Bashmet is only one of a number of up-and-coming modern virtuosos, the publicity he is getting can only be good for this once-neglected instrument.

Bashmet is a keen and engaging advocate of his instrument who believes that too few people appreciate its particular sound. "People say to me that the viola sounds sometimes like a violin, sometimes like a cello. But I think this is wrong," he says. "The viola has its own strong, very special, sound. In fact, to me, the cello or violin sometimes sounds like a viola. The viola is not just a middle instrument, but is the centre of gravity".

He is also an enthusiastic performer of transcriptions as well as the many viola works he has inspired. And, he believes, transcription does not always mean compromise with the originals: "Obviously when the composer writes, he hears in his mind one particular sound or instrument. But sometimes transcriptions can be better. The Bach Chaconne, for example, is better on the viola than the violin – it's more philosophical." He has played the Tertis transcription of the Elgar Cello Concerto, and thinks the viola version gives a different dimension.

His viola, a Testore, is surprisingly small for those of us used to charts on school walls that put the viola firmly halfway in size between the violin and cello. But he is adamant that the size of the viola is of minor importance. "I chose my viola because it had the best sound, and is comfortable to play, not because of the size. A good viola can be any size, maybe just a little bigger than a violin."

Size is a constant point of discussion among violists with no standard really having established itself: obviously a balance has to be struck between playability and depth of sound. The nearest to a standard is the Tertis size: he advocated 16 and five-eighths inches as the optimum size of the body along the back, whereas most modern instruments are 16-and-a-half inches. He himself played an enormous 18-inches model which was very deep as well as long.

Whatever the size, you'd be lucky to find a viola made by one of the masters: there are only a dozen Stradivariuses and four Guarneris left in the world – though not many were made to start with. But viola players are generally happier anyway to go for more modern instruments, which haven't been knocked about so much and provide just as rich a tone.

Juliette Barker makes violas in Cambridge and also teaches the art of viola making. She believes small is beautiful: her models are generally 16 and one sixteenth inches or 15 and five-eighths. "I do make a bigger one, but I don't really like the sound," she says. "The Tertis-size violas always sound like they're being played in a bathroom to me!" Work has been done on the acoustics of stringed instruments, particularly in Cambridge, but no-one is yet quite sure precisely how the sound quality of a viola and the size are connected. For string quartet players she makes slightly different instruments to those used by

Yuri Bashmet of Russia has established himself as the leading modern virtuoso of the viola, with many major new works written especially for him.

Sir William Walton wrote an excellent Viola Concerto – alongside his Violin Concerto it clearly shows the difference in character between the instruments.

orchestral players. "The orchestral violas are the big noisy ones, while the quartet models have more quality of sound, one hopes," she says, "though of course you can make quartet violas that sound perfectly well in an orchestra."

The materials used are the same as for a violin, and for most stringed instruments: spruce for the front of the soundbox, maple for the rest, ebony and rosewood for the fingerboard and the pegs. But the shape is not just a scaled-up violin. "Some makers have tried scaling up a violin, but I don't like the sound," says Barker. "I make the neck a little higher above the body so that the player's left hand doesn't bump into the body when playing high notes, and give it more bust and less hips in length, but not in width. The thickness of wood is exactly the same as on a violin, meaning it's comparatively thinner for its size".

She reckons to be a fast worker, producing a viola in about one hundred hours. A good modern instrument can cost around £2,000, though the variation in size and sound of the viola means a maker must know their buyers' requirements very precisely: "when you're selling violas you must be prepared for disappointments. Every player has a slightly different idea of what the sound should be, and so they can quite often pick up your favourite model and say they don't like the sound."

"With the violin you don't get this sort of variation," she says. "But it's this variety that makes viola making, and viola playing, so interesting."

The Finest Performers

Selected by Chris Bertram, viola player with the Birmingham Philharmonic

The most important name in the history of viola playing is Lionel Tertis. In a word, he was seminal: the man who made the viola into something like a popular instrument. Without Tertis there would be no Walton Concerto, and very probably little else. By showing what could be done technically he took the viola from obscurity to prominence, and made viola playing a viable occupation. His style would sound dated nowadays – he slid around quite a lot, which players tend not to do these days – but that's more a question of changing fashions than anything else. He left a large recording legacy but little of it appears now.

Also important in a slightly different way was the Scot William Primrose who added a new technical dimension to viola playing. He wrote a lot of treatises on technique, as well as a lot of exercise and study material, though made few recordings, and a lot of his music for development of technique has even been stolen by violinists!

Many violinists have tried playing the viola but the Israeli Pinchas Zukerman is one of the few who has succeeded. He has managed to bring across his virtuoso technique and innate feeling; it's a peculiarly Jewish sound, a very emotional kind of approach, like the violin sound of Jascha Heifetz.

Cecil Aronowitz was a South African particularly strong in chamber music and played as the Amadeus Quartet's fifth player when they performed quintet music. He was an excellent technician.

Of the modern players the Japanese Nobuko Imai and the Russian Yuri Bashmet stand out. Both are making a new virtuoso tradition and giving composers the chance to write new music for excellent players. Bashmet's association with the composer Alfred Schnittke has already produced a concerto and various chamber works, for example.

The Best CD Recordings

Chosen by Chris Bertram

A good place to start is the Bach *Brandenburg Concerto* No. 6 which features two violas instead of the more usual violins. It shows the subtle difference between Bach's violin and viola writing. There are dozens of versions of the *Brandenburg*s. Try the Academy of St Martin in the Fields under Sir Neville Marriner (Philips 400 076/7-2).

The Mozart *Sinfonia concertante* for violin, viola and orchestra is another of the few pre-twentieth-century pieces to show off the viola. The version played by Zukerman and Stern goes for the Mozart-as-romantic approach and works well, showing off the viola as a romantic instrument. It's also a good example of a violin player playing the viola and actually succeeding (Sony CD 36692).

The Walton Viola Concerto is probably the most successful of all modern works for the instrument. A tuneful and lyrical piece very much in a twentieth-century romantic style, it's extremely difficult, and with a lot of performers it shows. Nigel Kennedy's version is the best-known on CD, though it's debatable how successful his transition from the violin is (EMI CDC7 49628-2).

An interesting modern piece is Vaughan Williams's *Flos Campi* for viola, small chorus and small orchestra. It's based on the Song of Songs from the Bible and each of its five movements is headed by a quotation from it. It's the composer in a strange mood; there are some slightly odd noises and interesting polytonal effects. The Frederick Riddle recording on CD comes with Vaughan Williams's Viola Suite (Chandos CHAN6545).

Lots of music has been arranged for the viola, but the Brahms Viola Sonatas were arranged from his clarinet sonatas by Brahms himself and are a comparatively rare example of genuine nineteenth-century solo viola music. There are CD versions of this by Nobuko Imai (Chandos CHAN8550) and Yuri Bashmet (Olympia OCD175).

Meanwhile, one of the best known modern works, Schnittke's Viola Concerto, is available on an RCA CD played by the charismatic Russian player Yuri Bashmet (RCA RD60446).

THE CELLO

The most evocative and expressive instrument of all

Pablo Casals was one of the finest cello virtuosos who has ever lived, and established it as a solo instrument.

"The cello," says the composer Jonathan Harvey, "is very anthropomorphic. It has the size and shape of a human being, more than any other instrument, and matches the male and female voice range almost exactly. So it is a very direct form of communication, like someone expressing themselves. It's not just 'singing'; that's the great nineteenth-century cliché of cello music. The cello can do much more than that. It can be a rough, rhythmical thing, or a folkloric peasant instrument, or a gourmet of acoustical curiosities."

Perhaps it is this expressiveness that makes some cellists notorious for their histrionics while playing. Some virtuosos such as János Starker remain impassive in the face of the most traumatic parts of the Dvorak Concerto, while others writhe around constantly in a mixture of agony and ecstasy.

The cello is currently enjoying something of a boom, in repertoire, recording and playing, with plenty of excellent young players around. Yet the cello was not thought of as a solo instrument until relatively recently. Johannes Brahms was amazed by Dvorak's Cello Concerto when he heard it in 1895: "If only I'd known it was capable of that!" he is reported to have said. "I would have written a concerto myself."

The cello has always been a vital part of the orchestra, filling out the bass-lines above the double-basses, and a mainstay of the string quartet or piano trio; but until the end of the nineteenth century it was rarely used in sonatas or solo music. The Solo Cello Suites of J S Bach are an early landmark in the repertoire, and a surprising one in many ways, because as an Italian instrument the cello was usually passed over by German composers in favour of the viola da gamba. But Bach's musical intelligence gave the cello six pieces that are still a tremendous musical feat of writing and playing.

The baroque cello of Bach's time was one of a number of low-pitched strings; Bach himself uses the viola da gamba, violone and cello all together in one of the *Brandenburg* concertos – an odd mix to today's ears. It was roughly the same size as today's instrument, but with a less sharply angled neck, lower bridge, and lower tension gut strings which give a warmer sound with a more articulate attack at the beginning of a note – perfect for the insistent, almost mechanical rhythms of much baroque music. (The cello didn't take on steel strings, which give a better sustain, more suited to the singing lines of romantic music, until the 1920s.) The baroque cello didn't have the modern-day spike either – that came at the end of the nineteenth century. Players sat with their knees apart and ankles together, cradling the instrument on their calves.

The eighteenth century saw several major cello concertos by Boccherini, Haydn, C P E Bach, and Vivaldi, who wrote nearly two dozen. The instrument was constantly used in chamber music, especially in the string quartet that had been established by Haydn. But the early nineteenth century saw a tailing off of the repertoire. As with many other instruments, the surviving solo music is mainly written by player-composers. The cello equivalent of the Chopin Preludes for piano are the 48 Etudes by David Popper of Germany, who wrote many small cello pieces that are encountered by every cellist in every conservatoire in the world sooner or later. His *Dance of the Elves* is a favourite encore piece, and seems to end

Brinkwells, the summer refuge of Sir Edward Elgar, where he wrote his famous Cello Concerto in 1919.

Mstislav Rostropovich, the famous Russian cellist, whose cello was once owned by Napoleon and still bears his spur marks.

every Wigmore Hall debut recital.

The early 1800s were a time of great instrument development. Woodwinds were being radically redesigned, and strings were being made louder and brighter to fill the new larger concert halls. The bow changed shape, taking a curve which gave it higher tension and made possible a greater range of effects on string instruments such as bouncing the bow. The vocal qualities of the new brighter cello made it ideal for the romantic concerto which expressed the conflict between the individual and society, but it wasn't until the time of the Dvorak Cello Concerto that the instrument was taken up by composers. The amount of cello pieces from the nineteenth century that remain in the repertoire is really very small: a Schumann Concerto, the *Rococo Variations* by Tchaikovsky, two Brahms Sonatas but not really very much else.

Interest in the cello during the twentieth century was stimulated by virtuosos such as Pablo Casals and Emanuel Feuermann. Through their flawless technique and championing of repertoire they inspired composers to write new works for the instrument and so opened up the range of music available. Casals in particular brought cello technique forward: he opened out his shoulders, freeing out expressive possibilities for the players. Ironically, although Casals did more than anyone to create modern cello music, he didn't care for it very much and usually refused to play music of anything but the previous two centuries. However, it didn't stop Schoenberg writing a Concerto for him.

A landmark for the cello is the solo Sonata by Zoltán Kodály, which was championed by János Starker from an early age and stretched the instrument's technical possibilities. Cello concertos and sonatas became a standard task for a composer, and Mstislav Rostropovich was behind the writing of major works by Prokofiev, Shostakovich and Britten, who wrote three solo sonatas as well as a *Cello Symphony*. And with the recent interest in authentic music has come a revival of the baroque cello, with players such

Jacqueline Du Pré had an instinctive approach to phrasing which worked to best effect in her legendary recording of the Elgar Cello Concerto. Her career was tragically cut short by multiple sclerosis.

as Anner Bylsma playing works of the Bachs and other early composers on the instruments they were written for, or on copies of them.

Jonathan Harvey, Professor of Music at Sussex University, has written many solo and orchestral pieces for the cello including a recent concerto. "The main problem in writing for the cello is that you're limited to one line or spread chords," he says. "There's little harmonic richness as there is with ensemble or piano writing." But on the plus side he points to the extraordinary range of the cello, from the A below middle C to the E two octaves above it – and higher, if the composer wishes. "The cello can actually go higher than a violin, right up to the top note of piano, because it's very easy and natural to play up there. The higher you go the more of the bow sound you get, so it has a very ethereal quality. It has the quality of transforming the vocal melody into something more like refined thought. So the cello can have many different personalities: romantic, warm, human and dramatic, or bright, literary, cold sounds of a more celestial world."

Despite the bright sound and penetrating quality the cello can bring to melodic lines, as shown in any Rostropovich performance, there can be problems of balance, with the cello being swamped by the other instruments. "Few cello concertos – Elgar and Saint-Saëns's are examples – avoid the problem of balance," says Harvey. "What I did in my Concerto was to write very lightly andkeep a group of light high bright instruments surrounding soloists – harp,vibraphone, glockenspiel and so on."

The Elgar Cello Concerto is one of the most popular classical pieces of all time, and at one period in 1988 occupied the top three places in the classical charts. It is an emotional farewell to the old order that Elgar had seen destroyed by the First World War, and found its supreme interpreter in Jacqueline Du Pré. Her instinctive approach to phrasing worked better with some composers than others, but was perfect for the Elgar Concerto; two of her recordings, one directed by Sir John Barbirolli and the other by her husband Daniel Barenboim, were among the top three recordings, a feat that has never been surpassed.

Du Pré was lucky enough to own one of the world's 50 or so Stradivarius cellos, the Davidov, donated to her by an anonymous benefactor. Her instrument is now used by American cellist Yo Yo

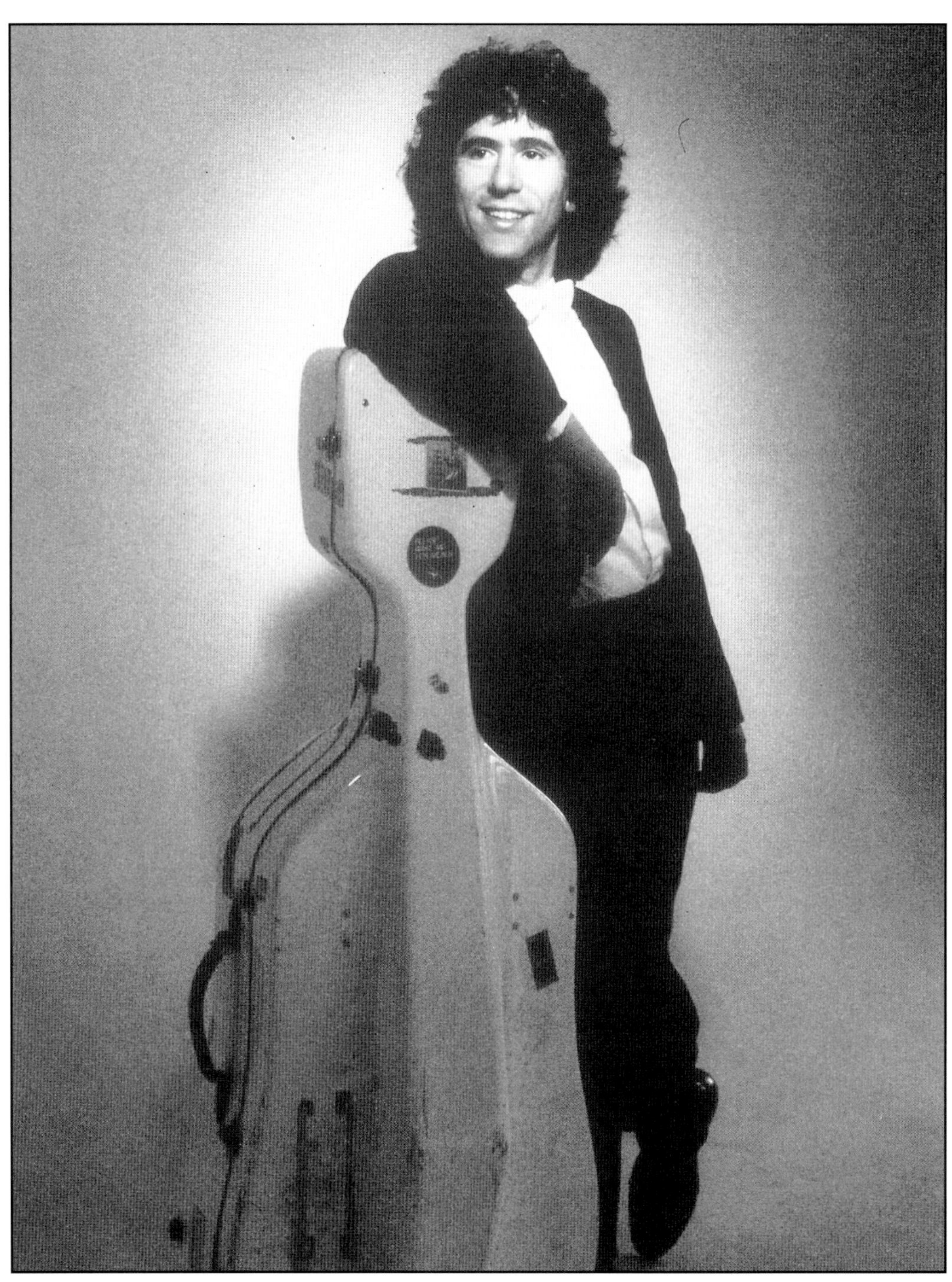

Stephen Isserlis is one of the best young players in the world, whose repertoire stretches from the standards to modern works by composers such as John Tavener.

Ma, who is one of the major modern players; other Strad-owning virtuosi include Rostropovich, whose Duport Stradivarius still bear marks reliably thought to be made by Napoleon's spurs! But whether played on a Strad or not, the diversity and scope of the modern repertoire – plus the ever-increasing technical brilliance of performers – is making the cello one of the most exciting and rewarding instruments to be playing in the 1990s.

THE FINEST PERFORMERS

Chosen by Neil Heyde, cellist with the Shiva Nova Group

Pablo Casals has to be first in the list. He established the cello as a solo instrument and championed the early repertoire, playing J S Bach's Solo Suites before anyone was doing the Violin Solo Partitas or Sonatas. He made lots of recordings – many of them, unfortunately, when he was old, which don't give a flattering account of his tone; but his early 1920s recordings on RCA are stunning. His technique was flawless, as was that of Emanuel Feuermann – the cellist's cellist, whose playing perfection was cut short by his early death during a routine operation.

Of current artists, Mstislav Rostropovich has done a lot to stimulate the twentieth-century interest in the cello. He's now making a career as a conductor, but as a cellist has been responsible for five major Britten pieces plus works by Shostakovich, Penderecki and Dutilleux, as well as inspiring many others indirectly by his championing of the modern repertoire. He has a huge, very Russian sound, very energetic. Paul Tortelier on the other hand had a French sound, thinner, slightly nervy perhaps, but with plenty of energy. He is an amazing player with a huge number of recordings.

The modern cellist's cellist is probably János Starker (b. 1924). With his technical perfection he was able to champion the Kodály Sonata for Solo Cello, a big and nasty piece which defeats many top-class players; Starker plays it effortlessly. He has also had a big impact as a teacher.

Finally Anner Bylsma, the Dutch cellist, has done a lot of excellent work on the baroque cello. He was principal cello with the Concertgebouw Orchestra and did the first baroque cello recordings of the J S Bach suites and the C P E Bach concertos.

THE BEST CD RECORDINGS

Selected by Neil Heyde

The major breakthrough of the century was Kodály's Sonata for Solo Cello (Delos DE1015). The recording by Janos Starker is amazing and shows what the cello is capable of. Starker made the piece what it was and has been playing it since he was 15.

J S Bach's Solo Cello Suites are a must for any collection, and Anner Bylsma's disc on Sony, on a period instrument, is wonderful playing and a very personal interpretation (Sony CD48047, two discs).

Pablo Casals's reissued Dvorak and Elgar Concertos has to be *the* Casals disc (EMI CDH7 63498-2). It shows his leanness of sound – a surprise to the modern listener. His Elgar is interesting if you know the work already, but you wouldn't recommend this as a first buy. The Dvorak has little rubato or vibrato and is emotional but unsentimental; it comes across very well.

A vintage 1920s recording on Biddulph shows the fluidity and technical perfection of Emanuel Feuermann in Strauss's *Don Quixote* and Bloch's *Schelomo* (Biddulph LAB042). Where Casals's playing is definitely from another era, Feuermann sounds modern.

THE BASS

The keystone of the orchestra

Everyone can sympathise with double-bass players. Dragging around a six-foot-tall instrument as wide as a water-butt clearly demands a lot of hard physical work. Even playing it is an effort.

But size is only the start of the bassist's problems. There isn't really a standard double-bass; they come with three, four or five strings, with or without key-work that can extend the length of the lowest string, are used in a bewildering variety of tunings, and have to cope with music written in three different clefs, sometimes written in the same key as it sounds, sometimes not. There are even two very different types of bow.

The confusion reflects the varied ancestry of the instrument. All sorts of very deep string instruments roughly the size of a man are known from at least the fifteenth century, appearing in dozens of different tunings, with anything from three to six strings, and under a variety of names such as 'violone'. It wasn't until the mid eighteenth century that double-basses became a fixed part of the orchestra, and when they did they were often positioned so that a bass and cello shared the same stand.

Harmony is built from the bottom up, so the basses, with their low range, took a crucial role in the orchestra. But few solo works appeared before 1800. Joseph Haydn wrote some solo bass parts into his symphonies, such as in Nos. 6–8, and the four years after 1765 saw a bass boom in which nearly 30 concertos were written by names such as Haydn, Vanhal, Sperger and Dittersdorf.

Mozart's contribution to the solo bass repertoire is, typically, surrounded by legend. His aria *Per questo bella mano,* K612, of 1791 for bass and double-bass demands some extremely difficult lines from the instrumentalist. It is said that Mozart made the bass part so absorbing for the dedicatee, Friedrich Pischelberger, as a diversion because Mozart was chasing Mrs Pischelberger at the time. The work is for a five-string bass with 'Austrian tuning', one of the more popular standards of the time. Pischelberger himself contributed many works to the solo repertoire and with his contemporary Johannes Sperger, who wrote 18 concertos and 24 sonatas, brought solo bass playing to new heights.

But the bass didn't take off as a solo instrument in England until the nineteenth century, with the arrival of the Italian Domenico Dragonetti (1763–1846). A friend of Haydn, Beethoven, Hummel, Spohr and Liszt, he was an essential part of any musical event in London for over 50 years. A popular and respected figure because of his great musical gifts and amiable personality, he could command £150 a performance – a sum which could then buy a large house in the centre of London. He had some curious interests outside of music too: at his flat in Drury Lane he collected life-sized dolls, some of which he used to take out with him. His works may sound a little trite now, but his playing was praised for its accuracy and power. The bass part in Beethoven's Ninth Symphony is even more challenging and rewarding than those in his other symphonies, for it was written with Dragonetti in mind.

Dragonetti's fellow Italian Giovanni Bottesini (1821–1889) was the next great bass virtuoso. His many compositions for the instrument, including two concertos, are generally thought to be better than Dragonetti's, and he brought the repertoire on. His playing ability was so astonishing, particularly in its use of high harmonics, that he earned the title "the

Giovanni Bottesini was one of the great bass virtuosos of the last century, and wrote a great many compositions for the solo instrument.

Paganini of the double-bass". He also wrote an important tutor for the instrument. Bottesini was a music director and conductor, an associate of Verdi who was important enough to conduct the first performance of his opera *Aida* in Cairo.

Another double-bass player-conductor was Sergei Koussevitzky (1874–1951) who for many years was conductor of the Boston Symphony Orchestra. Like Bottesini, he took up the bass because it was one of the few instruments with scholarship vacancies at his conservatoire. He wrote some good if 'salony' pieces for the bass, with help from his compatriot Glière; his Concerto for bass is one of the few standard solo items for the instrument, though his own recital programmes consisted largely of transcriptions of works like Bruch's *Kol Nidrei* or Mozart's Bassoon Concerto.

Twentieth-century contributions to the solo repertoire include few pieces by well-known composers: there is a Sonata by Hindemith, a Concerto by Henze and a Duet for bass and trombone by Elgar. More recently, the American bass player Gary Karr has brought the solo instrument to a wide audience through many television appearances, and bass playing technique has developed considerably since the 1950s. Perhaps the most familiar image of the bass now for many music listeners is in jazz, where the plucked-string technique of players like Niels-Henning Pederson (who unusually uses all four right hand fingers to pluck his instrument) contributes a combination of harmonic foundation and percussion to small jazz groups.

But to concentrate on the soloists is to miss the point of the double-bass. It is not really a solo instrument; like the bread base of a pizza, it's vital to what goes on top but isn't very appetising by itself. Robin McGee, double-bassist with the London Sinfonietta, is worried that too many young players come to the bass treating it as a solo instrument, an approach that doesn't work in orchestral playing. He points to bass lines in Puccini operas as examples, such as *La Bohème* and *Madama Butterfly*, which are crucial to the music but, not being soloistic in character, can lose players who think too individually.

McGee believes that the best bass writing occurs in orchestral music, and that the character of the instrument comes out most effectively when it is in the context of the orchestra. For example, the bass solo in Stravinsky's *Pulcinella*, Strauss's *Salome*, Prokofiev's *Lieutenant Kijé*, the "Elephant" in Saint-Saëns's *Carnival of the Animals*, the solo in the slow movement of Mahler's First Symphony, the lumbering ox-cart "Bydlo" in Mussorgsky's *Pictures at an Exhibition*... the list is endless. One of the best examples of bringing out the bass's character is in the opera *Albert Herring*, where Britten associates the bass with a policeman character in a typically craftsmanlike piece of writing.

Playing the bass needs a sound musicality, but the instrument's sheer size demands physical strength too. Merely playing the right notes is difficult enough (the hand can only span one tone, making a scale passage quite a strain as the fingers stamp across the strings) and making solo lines project is very hard work. Clearly this presents problems to the young player – hence the recent introduction of the mini-bass, about as large as a cello, which can be played successfully by children as young as seven.

Gary Karr is the foremost modern showman for the solo bass.

One thing the mini-bass doesn't prepare the player for is the system of levers on some classical basses. This extends the length of the bottom string by a foot or so: a lever normally keeps the string pressed down to make its length the same as the other strings (and sound an E) but by pressing keys with the left hand the player can sound any note down to C. Even without the levers, the bass has a range of over five octaves, making it one of the few instruments that can successfully be played as a quartet. The Berlin Philhar-monic Orchestra has a good bass quartet, and there are some interesting pieces for the genre by Glasser and Ruswick.

The tuning of the bass has standardised now but solo pieces often call for different tunings to make them playable. Worse, there is a tradition of solo pieces being played with all the strings taken up a tone to make them sound brighter; thus, the orchestral parts might be scored in E major, while the bass part is scored in D major. A player with perfect pitch thus has the distressing experience of playing one key and hearing another.

It raises the question of whether all this effort to make the double-bass a solo instrument is really necessary. For the instrument is at its most effective when it is laying the harmonic foundation of an orchestral work; the bass is best celebrated not as a thing in itself, but as an essential part of the structure of Western music.

THE FINEST PERFORMERS

Chosen by Robin McGee (bass player with the London Sinfonietta) and Angela Schofield (co-principal bass with the English National Opera)

Gary Karr of America is unique: a real showman who has popularised the bass, though to some extent, when you've seen his act once…

In Britain Duncan McTier has developed into our most outstanding soloist since winning the second Isle of Man Festival a few years ago, and actually manages to make his living as a solo performer. Adrian Beers of the English Chamber Orchestra is just about the last of the generation who worked a lot with Britten and Pears at Aldeburgh. The late Stuart Knussen was a good sound orchestral player whose musical perception within the orchestra was exceptional.

Someone who has made great contributions to the bass in various fields is Rodney Slatford who popularised the mini-bass, started the Isle of Man Bass Festival in the early 1980s, and has published lots of valuable bass music through his company Yorke Publishing.

Two important European bassists are Ludwig Streicher, principal of the Berlin Philharmonic Orchestra for years, and Frantisek Posta, principal of the Czech Philharmonic Orchestra, who had a good solid view of the bass in orchestral music.

The Best CD Recordings

Selected by Robin McGee and Angela Schofield

On a CD called "Smoke Gets in Your Eyes" you can hear Duncan McTier's phenomenal playing of Glière's *Tarantelle*, making worthwhile music out of an ordinary piece (Denon DC8124). Some of Bottesini's solo bass works can be heard on a Koch Schwann CD including his *Grande Concerto in quattro tempi*, played by Stoll and Günther (Koch Schwann 311042).

But the bass is an orchestral instrument rather than a solo instrument. The best double-bass section in the world – that of the Czech Philharmonic Orchestra – is a must; their recording of the opera *The Bartered Bride* by their fellow-Czech Bedrich Smetana is a real showcase for them (Supraphon 10 3511-2). Great orchestral bass playing can also be heard on Mravinsky's versions of the Tchaikovsky Symphonies with the Leningrad Philharmonic Orchestra (Deutsche Grammophon 419 745-2).

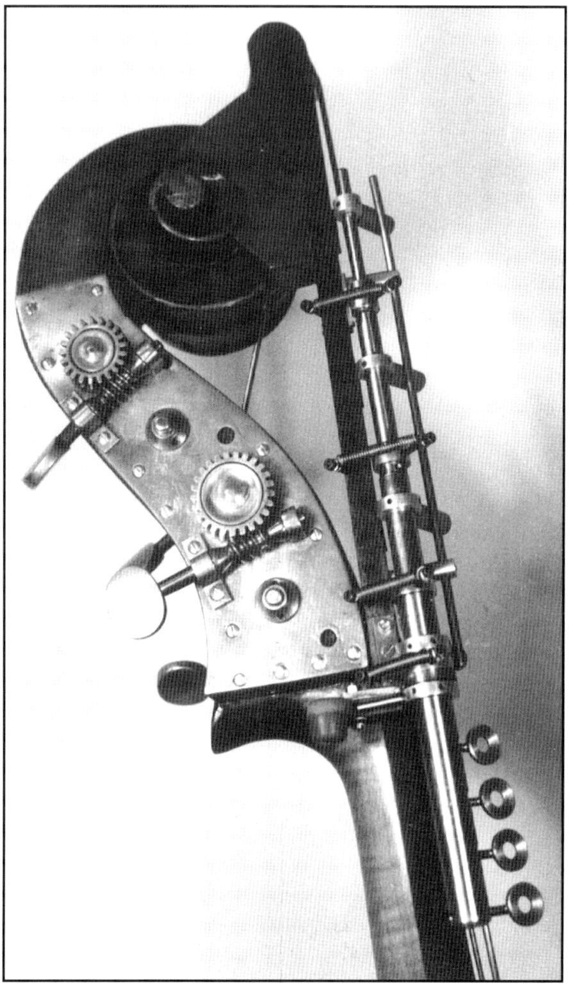

The extended lower string of a bass can make it possible for the player to reach right down to a low C.

Finally, Robin McGee is far too modest to pick his own London Sinfonietta doing the "Elephant" from Saint-Saëns's *Carnival of the Animals* as an example of how the bass's character comes out in orchestral playing (Decca 414 460-2).

THE FLUTE

One of the best-loved instruments of the orchestra, now enjoying its third golden age

James Galway and his famous golden flute has played everything from popular chart hits (John Denver's "Annie's Song") to avant-garde modern works.

The pattern of sound produced by the flute, as an oscilloscope trace shows, is just about the purest tone you can get: a smooth, undulating wave, unspiked by mixtures of higher notes. Its simple sound, so easy on the ear – coupled with the instrument's extraordinary agility in handling fast runs – has charmed listeners since the emergence of the flute in the sixteenth century. But somehow it has never quite made it as a serious solo instrument, despite being an essential part of any orchestra.

"It's an intensely vocal instrument," says the flautist Susan Milan, "which can be like a coloratura opera singer one minute and a simple melodic instrument the next. It has a great palette of tone-colours and an enormous range. It appears to be an easy instrument to play at first, and many children can pick it up very quickly – but at the high end it has the greatest technical demands of any wind instrument."

The flute has had three main incarnations, each associated with a "golden age". In the Renaissance period various flute-like instruments were around. Those blown from the end became the modern recorder; those from the side the modern flute, but they were all essentially simple pipes, with holes which the player would cover with the fingers to make the notes. In the 1650s Jacques Hotteterre made the significant adv-ance of splitting the side-blown flute into three parts: the head, with the mouthpiece;

Frederick the Great of Prussia found time away from his royal duties to write a great number of flute sonatas and concertos (or perhaps not…).

the body, with most of the holes; and the foot, with a few of the lowest holes.

It had a far-reaching effect. Holes on a flute are not bored perpendicular to the axis of the instrument. The tops are in a place convenient for the fingers; the bottoms, inside the tube, are in a place to make the notes the right pitch. Reaching inside the single-piece flute to bore these holes to the right skew was difficult, but with the three-piece set-up, it was much easier. This apparently simple device had the effect of turning the flute from a military and folk pipe into a genuine musical instrument. The sound quality improved drastically and, with the addition of a single key to add the one note (D sharp) that couldn't be achieved by combinations of fingering, the flute could tackle the sort of wide-ranging music being written by the baroque composers. In the early years of the eighteenth century Hotteterre wrote the first flute tutor and the first solo flute music had appeared, written by Michel de LaBarre.

It was the beginning the first golden age: that of the baroque flute. In the eighteenth century it was the instrument for a gentleman to be seen playing – or at least, holding, as any portrait of a fashionable aristocratic family of the period will show. Such was the its popularity that whole operas were arranged for solo flute, and one band, the "Gentlemen's Concerts" was founded in Manchester in 1774 consisting solely of 26 flutes.

Frederick the Great of Prussia (1712–1786) was a keen flute player, and one of the select band of composing royalty, writing countless flute sonatas and concertos (though some say he wrote only the flute parts, the rest being filled in by his court organist, who was a pupil of J S Bach). Frederick's flute teacher Quantz (1697–1773) composed something like 300 flute concertos and 200 flute sonatas and wrote a treatise on flute playing that was still in print over 170 years later. (His pronouncements are so often taken as gospel that a sentence beginning "Quantz says…" is bound to bring groans from many flute players). Frederick's appetite for music is said to have ceased in his sixties – possibly due to losing his flute teacher, but more probably his teeth; it is virtually impossible to achieve the right lip

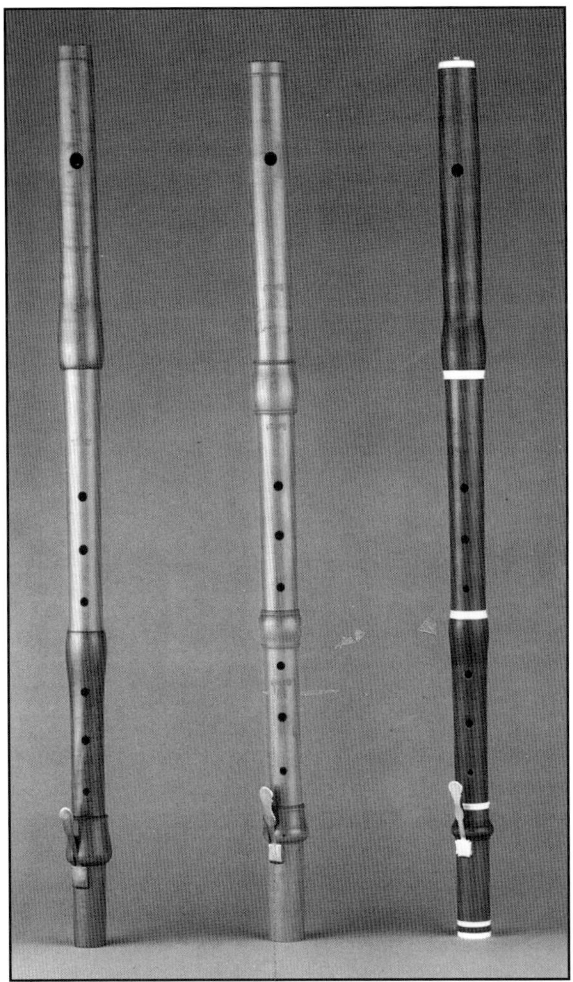

Before the mid-1800s, flute keywork was virtually non-existent; the tone produced was thinner than that of today's instruments and some notes sounded out of tune.

position to play the flute – the embouchure – without dental support.

The flute boom was particularly strong in the French courts; and if every man had a flute, every young lady had a harp. The two instruments have gone together ever since, with composers from Mozart to Ravel writing for compositions for flute and harp. Bach, Handel and Haydn all wrote several chamber pieces for the flute, and Bach's Suite in B minor – effectively a flute concerto – is a very familiar piece today.

However, as musical writing became more and more adventurous through the late eighteenth and early nineteenth centuries, the flute's lopsided sound began to show up. The problem was that different keys had a different sound. Sharp keys sounded brighter and brighter the further away the composer strayed from C major; flat keys became more veiled and muted. Thus a phrase that modulated halfway through from a sharp key to a flat key when played on the flute would have a sudden change of feeling that the composer might not have wanted. Mozart has a reputation for not liking the flute, though it didn't stop him writing two concertos, a double concerto for flute and harp, and three quartets for flute and strings to commissions. But his misgivings were shared by other major composers, who generally ignored the instrument, or – like Beethoven or Schubert – wrote a few chamber pieces.

As the nineteenth century got under way, the flute was seen as an old-fashioned instrument, played by enthusiastic amateurs, possessing a repertoire enormously broad but lacking in depth: hundreds and hundreds of flashy parlour-pieces from composing flute-players that showed off the agility of the instrument but did little else. The solo flute, like most other wind instruments, was in decline, and the golden age was over.

The increasing mechanical skills being developed in the early nineteenth century came to the rescue. The simple amateur's flute, still basically a wooden tube with holes, needed some engineering to bring it up to date. Theobald Boehm was a German flute player, silversmith and engineer – just the right combination of skills to redesign the instrument. Discarding the trial-and-error approach used by his predecessors, he used his technical design skills to work out on paper the ideal positions of all the holes so that the flute would have an even sound across all of its range. Then he devised a system of keys that would sit comfortably under the player's fingers and work a mechanism to close up specific holes, often nowhere near the position of the finger. Only then, in the early 1830s, did he attempt to build the instrument.

He refined his new flute over the next 15 years. He used metal, partly for the brighter sound, but mainly because it was a much more reliable material than wood, less prone to cracking and warping. He retained the three-part design, but made the central part, with most of the keywork, cylindrically bored instead of conically, evening out the sound of a scale. He had the head joint cylindrically bored too, but made the end parabolic, to focus the sound down the tube like a headlamp reflector.

The final model, the Boehm flute of 1847, is virtually identical to the flutes of today, and could cope convincingly with the increasingly complicated music of the romantic period. Yet it didn't take off immediately. After all, Boehm was not alone; there were dozens of other makers trying to do what he was doing, all in different ways, and many of their creations were so laughably impractical that yet another new flute was bound to be treated with suspicion. Also the post-Mozart scepticism of the instrument by composers had still to be overcome. Neither the Germans nor the English took to his flute, preferring the old wooden models; it was in France that the second golden age started.

French flute makers began switching to the new design, and Louis Lot, the flute-making equivalent of Stradivarius, made instruments of such high quality many of his 1850s models are still being used today. Paul Taffanel (1844–1908) was the first serious flute soloist to use the Boehm flute, and was part of the big revival that brought the new improved instrument to the attention of major composers again, in France at least. Debussy showed what could be done with the flute, not only as an unaccompanied solo instrument (with his short solo piece *Syrinx*) but also as part of the orchestral palette of sounds: his famous *Prélude à l'après-midi d'un faune* starts with the liquid tones of the lower register of the Boehm flute, setting the perfect atmosphere for the piece. He also wrote for the flute as a chamber piece with his Sonata for flute, viola and harp, as did Ravel. French players toured and emigrated to America, taking the new instrument and music with them, and the instrument was established again. It was a French player, Marcel Moyse (1889–1984) who pioneered the recording of flute

The nimble sounds of the **piccolo** have been used to great effect by symphonic composers such as Shostakovich and Sir Malcolm Arnold.

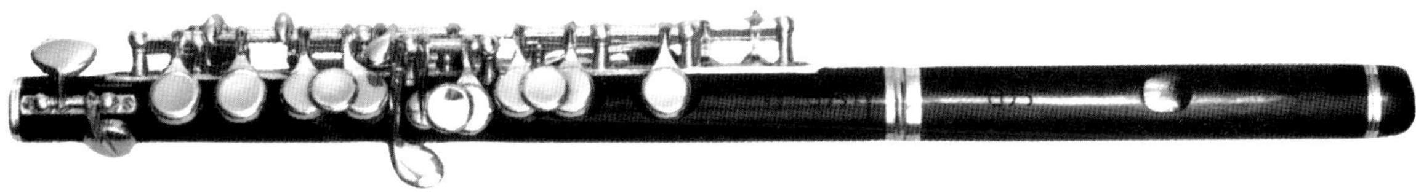

William Bennett may not be as famous a name as James Galway but he has established a very high reputation among flute players as a superb artist and technician.

pieces. The instrument's clear and simple sound quality made the flute an ideal candidate for recording on early machinery, and Moyse recorded prolifically.

The French players were developing flute technique all the time in the early part of this century. For example, vibrato had never been a strong feature of flute playing, and the baroque flute is usually played with straight, vibratoless tones. Moyse, however, influenced by the technique of singers he'd worked with, incorporated vibrato into his playing. The strong mouthpiece of the Boehm-style flute made it easier for the player to make an embouchure, and the more relaxed lip positions made for a smoother, swirlier, more flexible sound. Some players describe it as an "art nouveau" sound, in contrast to the strong but stiff character of the traditional style. Britain, as usual, lagged behind these developments, with the wooden flute still being more popular until the 1940s.

The third golden age – not that the second has ever really ended – came with the advent of mass-produced flutes in the 1960s and 1970s. An inexpensive Japanese model can be bought today for the same price as a hi-fi system. The explosion in the number of players in the last 25 years has made the flute one of the most familiar instruments at all levels from school up to recording orchestras; the British Flute Society is thriving with thousands of members, regular newsletters and dozens of events through the year from masterclasses to concerts. The flute even has its obligatory media star in the shape of Irish player James Galway, who had a hit in the pop singles charts with Annie's Song, though his fame is due as much to shrewd management as to his undoubted ability.

Yet though the flute has established itself as a vital part of the orchestra, the solo repertoire is still surprisingly thin. Virtually every orchestral composer this century has highlighted the flute in their work somewhere: Stravinsky's *Petrushka*; Shostakovich's Fifth and Fifteenth Symphonies; Prokofiev's bird in *Peter and the Wolf*; Ravel's "La Flûte enchantée" from *Shéhérazade*... the list goes on and on. But concertos, or even substantial chamber pieces, are another matter. Nielsen is one of the few symphonists to have written a flute concerto; Jolivet also did one, and Ibert's sums up the French school of the late nineteenth and early twentieth century. Messiaen has written a short piece, Boulez a *Sonatine*, and Martinu a good Sonata, but that's about it: no solo works by Britten, Shostakovich, Tippett, Sibelius or the rest.

Strange, because composer John McCabe, whose Flute Concerto was premiered by James Galway in 1990, says that it's a relatively easy instrument to write for. When Galway asked him to write a flute concerto, McCabe had the idea of expressing the character of spume crashing out from waves breaking on the sea shore, and found that the fast patterns of notes he heard in his head were quite playable on the flute.

"Of course there are secrets with any instrument that only a player knows about," he says, "and you have a slight problem with balance, because the flute can easily get drowned by the woodwind. But otherwise it's fairly straightforward. I had the notes firmly in my mind before I wrote them down. Jimmy checked that the patterns were playable and suggested a few things, but didn't change much." One of the changes Galway did persuade McCabe to make was to have the final few bars, originally written for the very lowest register of the flute, to be played on the alto flute, which is pitched a fifth lower than the normal instrument – thus giving the concerto the unusual property of ending on a different instrument from the one on which it began.

Galway's solid gold instrument is almost as well-known as he is. Flutes have been made out of various metals – everything from steel to silver, gold and platinum, on the basis that the denser metals give a brighter tone – but flute maker Albert Cooper is sceptical. "I don't think it makes any difference," he says. "If there was a single best metal for the flute, it would have showed up by now, which simply isn't the case. It's all down to the shape of the head joint and cut of the mouthpiece that determines the sound, and you can get good and bad whatever the metal you use."

So crucial is the shape of the head joint – the keyless top third of the instrument that has the mouthpiece – that Cooper, who started working for famous makers Rudall Carte in 1938, now specialises exclusively in making head joints. "The Americans and Japanese do good mass-produced bodies with good keywork, but they can't mass-produce good head joints," he says. "That's all down to trial and error, and skill. You can't read it in a book." He stresses the importance of the head joint in determining the sound quality of the whole instrument: "You can put the same body with four different head joints," he says, "and it'll sound like four different instruments." Players who have come to buy a head joint for their flute, he says, always choose the loudest one, rather than the one with the best tone: "They say they just want the best quality of sound," he laughs, "and if I ask them to pick the best, they will do. But if they're buying, they always buy the loudest one!"

The modern flute doesn't have it all its own way. The revival of interest in authentic instruments in the 1980s has seen many flute players taking up the old wooden one-keyed baroque flute again for music of that period, with its totally different technique and tighter, recorder-like sound. Many compositions of the baroque period are available in modern or baroque flute versions, and the flute has been well represented been well represented on the CD catalogue since the medium's inception. On vinyl only the efforts of Jean-Pierre Rampal, who kept up t he recording of flute music in the 1950s and 1960s, saved the repertoire from sliding away from the listening public.

With hundreds of thousands of players worldwide, a healthy CD catalogue and a high musical profile, the flute – in both baroque and modern forms – is well established. Players and listeners must now hope that composers of the twenty-first century can make the solo repertoire match the orchestral and chamber repertoire in depth and breadth.

THE FINEST PERFORMERS

Chosen by Edward Blakeman, Chairman of the British Flute Society

Flute playing on records began early this century in the era of 78s with the great French flautists such as Philippe Gaubert and Marcel Moyse who remain models of all that is best in the art. Their resonant flexibility of tone and superb musicianship are preserved on a series of recordings recently remastered on CD. Since the advent of LPs the quicksilver sound and technique of Jean-Pierre Rampal has also exerted an enormous influence. Rampal is still going strong making new recordings on CD and some of his best earlier ones are also being reissued.

James Galway is the other flute star of our times who has done much to popularise the instrument and its music. There are many recordings to choose from, some of them variable, as his distinctive sound and style suit some pieces better than others, but there is certainly never any shortage of technical fireworks.

Another player who is exploring the flute repertoire with a growing list of fine recordings is Susan Milan, who displays a brilliant technique and a strongly vibrant tone. There are two players whose recordings I could not be without: Aurèle Nicolet and William Bennett. Nicolet produces the most bewitchingly beautiful flute sound allied to impeccable musicianship. And Bennett is unique. He never fails to amaze, delight, challenge, and inspire.

Meanwhile there is a whole world of flute playing – or rather the revival of an old world – on baroque instruments. The baroque flute has a delicately transparent tone and an intimate quality of music making which has quite transformed out perception of the early repertoire. Very much a taste worth acquiring. Bart Kuijken, Stephen Preston, Lisa Beznosiuk and Konrad Hünteler are some of the names to look out for.

THE BEST CD RECORDINGS

Selected by Edward Blakeman

The Bach Sonatas and Mozart Concertos are the mainstays of the eighteenth-century flute repertoire, and new and reissued recordings continue to appear. I think the baroque flute playing of Bart Kuijken is more thoughtful and stylish than most other current versions on CD, even though it was recorded in an over-resonant acoustic (Deutsche Harmonia Mundi RD77026, two discs). Jean-Pierre Rampal on the modern flute is perfectly suited to Mozart's elegant turns of phrase – French players have always famous for crisp articulation – and he is ably partnered by Lily Laskine in the sparkling Flute and Harp Concerto (Erato 2292-45832-2).

Sadly, flute music lapsed into the doldrums for much of the nineteenth century but a valuable new repertoire grew up around the French players of the time: Saint-Saëns and Fauré. William Bennett plays a selection of this music on a recital disc called "Celebration for Flute and Orchestra" (ASV CDDCA652).

French composers have continued to enrich the flute repertoire and Susan Milan gives polished performances of two of the most important twentieth-century concertos – by Ibert and Jolivet – on her recital disc "La Flûte enchantée", which also includes Frank Martin's thrilling *Ballade*.

For me, the greatest non-French twentieth-century concerto is the one by Nielsen, and Aurèle Nicolet brings out all its subtle qualities on a disc which also includes the Reinecke Concerto and the Divertimento by Busoni (Philips 412 728-2).

Martinu's Sonata is another indispensable gem of

Jean-Pierre Rampal is a modern master of the flute who has been recording for decades, during which time he has covered much of the instrument's repertoire.

the repertoire which deserves to be much better known. James Galway is in fine form here, and he also offers works by Dvorak and Jindrich Feld on the same disc (RCA RD87802). Finally, a fascinating glimpse back into the past is offered by "The Great Flautists". They are Philippe Gaubert, Georges Barrère, Adolphe Hennbains, René le Roy and Marcel Moyse. The music is by Bach, Gluck, Beethoven, Chopin and many others. Gaubert's performance of Debussy's "Le Petit Berger" and Moyse's of the Debussy Sonata for flute, viola and harp should not be missed (Pearl GEMMCD 9284/9302).

The Clarinet

The baby of the orchestra

Clarinet players, according to clarinettist Tony Pay, are very lucky. "The instrument has a very wide dynamic range, and a wonderful repertoire," he says, "possibly the best of the wind instruments. And it can claim at least equal fluency: there's practically nothing you can write that someone somewhere can't play. It's good for power and for variety of tone colours: it has at least three quite different-sounding registers. You can make them sound the same, or exploit the potential of differences."

But the expressivity and flexibility comes at a price. The clarinet is more difficult to play than most of its relatives in the woodwind family: a flute player can finger a low E, say, and just alter the blowing pressure to make it play a high E. But if a clarinettist fingers a low E and does the equivalent (opens the register key), the instrument plays the B above the high E: the clarinet 'overblows at the twelfth'. This causes headaches for the player – for whom the keying is more complicated than for other wind instruments – and also for the maker, because the construction of an instrument that will play low and high notes in tune is something of a compromise. It also means that notes in the middle register – the ones leap-frogged over by this overblowing at a twelfth – have to be made in other ways, often with awkward fingerings, giving the clarinet a slightly uneven sound. (Though a physicist might argue that a clarinet has a perfectly even sound: its cylindrical bore gives only even-numbered harmonics for any note.) More than most wind instruments, the tone produced by a player is as much a product of their anatomy as the instrument's; because the clarinet is effectively an open pipe at the mouthpiece end, the sound is affected by the shape and size of the player's mouth.

Distant ancestors of the clarinet were played in the ancient world. Very early music, such as the few surviving fragments of Greek music we have, has been played convincingly on the clarinet. Similar instruments, shaped like long clay pipes but made of wood and having a backward-facing reed on the mouthpiece, can be bought today in the markets of Egypt. The predecessor of the clarinet was a folk instrument called the chalumeau, but in about 1690 a Nuremberg maker, Johann Denner, evolved it into something approaching the modern instrument by adding a speaker-key to access the higher range of notes, and the clarinet was born. More keys were added, and in the eighteenth century the clarinet – an instrument never used by Bach or his contemporaries – gradually became accepted into serious music. An Antwerp organist called Faber included it in a Mass in 1720, and Jan Stamic wrote probably the earliest surviving concerto for a B flat clarinet somewhere around 1740–50. (Vivaldi had already written works for the C clarinet.) Orchestras in England, Scotland,

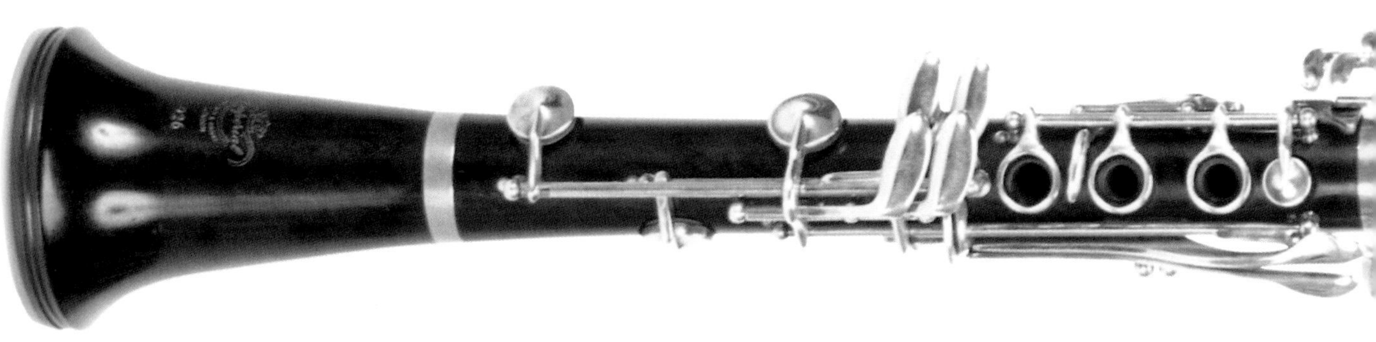

France and Germany gradually took up the clarinet in the mid 1700s. Mozart wrote approvingly to his father in 1778 of their "lordly effect", and included clarinets in his *Paris* Symphony, No. 31, of the same year. He also wrote a concerto, quintets, divertimenti and many other chamber works. His enthusiasm for the clarinet must have done a lot to establish it as an orchestral instrument; most other composers of the time, such as Haydn, had been using it much less.

The popularity of Mozart's music – much of it written for his friend and fellow freemason Anton Stadler – had the welcome effect of legitimising and hence standardising the design of the clarinet, which up till then had varied from maker to maker. Stadler and his clarinet maker, Lotz, had added more keys to extend the lower range of the instrument. This seven-keyed model became the standard, but more and more keys were added in the 1800s by Bärmann and Oehler. Their instrument was rationalised into a more complex, differently constructed clarinet after the Boehm system in 1842; the Boehm system became the norm in the orchestra in most countries, with the other German system persisting in German-speaking countries up to this day. There evolved a range of instruments, from the small, high-pitched E flat and D clarinets (used by Shostakovich in his symphonies) to the bass clarinet and basset horn (which Mozart calls for in the *Gran partita*). Richard Strauss uses virtually all of them in *Elektra*.

The clarinet enjoyed something of a boom in the early nineteenth century, and the repertoire began to expand. Often a virtuoso player would inspire a composer to write for the clarinet and the two would work closely together on the music, as Mozart had done with Stadler. For example Louis Spohr, working with Johann Hermstedt, wrote four concertos. Carl Maria von Weber contributed two Concertos, a *Concertino*, and a *Grand duo concertante* for clarinet and piano, one of the best showpieces for the instrument, inspired by Heinrich Bärmann, himself a composer for the clarinet. Weber's music is extremely virtuosic and exploits the deeper sounds in the lower register of the instrument very effectively. Brahms, in association with the player Richard Mühlfeld, wrote some of the best music for the clarinet: two sonatas, a trio and a quintet. A Swedish composer-clarinettist called Crusell evidently didn't need such collaboration and wrote three good concertos by himself. The clarinet had well and truly entered the mainstream of chamber and orchestral music; composers such as Beethoven, Schumann and Mendelssohn included the clarinet in their chamber music, but Mozart, Weber and Brahms were probably the three greatest exponents of clarinet writing.

Since then there have been sonatas and chamber works from most major composers: Strauss, Saint-Saëns, Debussy, Busoni, Berg, Poulenc, Reger and Bartók among others. In the twentieth century the

Benny Goodman wasn't just a consummate jazz player: he was a classically trained clarinettist good enough to have played the Mozart Concerto.

clarinet, with its great range and expressive capabilities, became a standard member of the jazz and swing band line-up; many composers were influenced by this new type of music, and Stravinsky's jazz-inspired *Ebony Concerto* for clarinet and swing band was written for the bandleader Woody Herman and premiered by him and his band in Carnegie Hall in 1946.

Benny Goodman (who also played much of the classical clarinet repertoire including Mozart's concerto with the New York Philhar-monic) was another jazz clarinettist to commission concertos from major classical composers such as Hindemith, Copland, Milhaud and Britten – though the Britten piece has had a bizarre history. While Britten was staying in America in the early 1940s, he was inspired to write a clarinet concerto by the playing of Goodman, who was urging composers to write works that would help him extend or break away from the jazz idiom. However, he only had time to write a single movement sketch, and in 1942 as he boarded the boat back to England, New York customs officials confiscated the manuscript. Britain was at war with Germany, and Britten was regarded as something of a subversive, having been involved with left-wing theatre groups in his youth. The officials therefore suspected that the untidy manuscript, obscured by crossings-out and comments, might contain coded messages to the Germans.

Britten was now busy with his opera *Peter Grimes*, and away from the inspiration of America, never got around to finishing the piece. But in 1990 the surviving fragment was orchestrated and reconstructed into a complete six-minute *Molto allegro* movement by Colin Matthews, and played at the Barbican in London. Nobody could detect any coded messages.

Other unpublished clarinet works are being revived from composers of all eras. Michael Bryant of the British Clarinet Society has been active in finding, and bringing back to life, forgotten masterpieces. He started it when he wanted to extend the repertoire available to the amateur – "you get six of you together to do the Poulenc Sextet, for example," he says, "and then you wonder what else there is to play." The joy comes, says Bryant, "when you find that some of the unpublished music is better than the published repertoire". He has recently resuscitated unpublished clarinet pieces by, among others, Reitz, Rheinberger, Reinecke and three works by the English composer Charles Stanford: the *Nonet* and the *Fantasies* for clarinet and string quartet.

"I knew about the Stanford *Nonet* because it's listed in some reference books on him," he says. "His music is kept at the University of Newcastle, so I checked with the librarian who sent me the manuscript." He collaborated with the Royal College of Music in 1987 to put on a concert which included the music. Bryant invited a few people from the record companies to hear the rediscovered work, and when they liked it, Hyperion agreed to make a recording, which was released in 1989. The Stanford *Fantasies* are something of a mystery; no-one knows why or for whom they were written, and they were not listed in any books on the composer. Bryant only heard about them when a student in San Antonio, whom he was helping to research his thesis, stumbled on them in the Newcastle archives and wrote telling Bryant of their existence. For other composers, unpublished manuscripts are often found languishing in collections, or are with their relatives.

The early forms of clarinet are being revived as well, as part of the resurgence of interest in period instruments. Daniel Bangham of Cambridge is one maker who has started producing repli-cas of early clarinets for players wishing to tackle music from the late 1700s and early 1800s. One such instrument, a seven-key Simiot replica, had two extra keys added for Tony Pay to tackle the complexity of the Weber concertos. In fact, Weber wrote it for a ten-keyed instrument, but as Bangham didn't have time to reconstruct one, Pay simply played the concertos on an instrument supposedly not capable of the music. "It was an amazing technical feat of skill," says Bangham. Most of his instruments are straight copies of existing instruments, but he is now constructing a basset clarinet – effectively a normal clarinet with extra keys to add two, possible four extra lower notes on to the bottom of the range. "The trouble is," says Bangham, "no basset clarinets exist now, so nobody really knows what they were like. People have travelled thousands of miles on the off-chance of seeing one, without success."

Critics of period instrument players would say this begs the question of why older, 'inferior' instruments should be rebuilt in the firstplace. "It's because the sound is very different,"says Bangham, "and the way you play the instruments has chan-ged. If you play Mozart or Weber on instru-ments that don't behave the way they expected them to, you're forced into the wrong style; you don't have to break and pause and tune in a way for which the music was written."

Tony Pay, one of the foremost players of period clarinets, agrees. As with many instruments, more

Jack Brymer has established himself as the elder statesman of clarinet playing, with a great list of recordings as soloist and orchestral player.

Emma Johnson is one of Britain's rising young clarinettists whose enthusiasm has made a lot of converts to classical music.

recent models which produce sounds loud enough to reach to the back of large modern concert halls are not necessarily better than older instruments in a musical sense. "Roughly speaking, the older instrument is gentler sounding," he says, "and also more flexible in a certain way – more adapted to playing phrases, rather than producing large dynamics. It's like using a foil instead of a broad sword, or driving a Bugatti instead of a Ferrari; what it loses in power it gains in expressivity. Because the fingerings are simple, it means there are more subtleties of tone colour possible. It's nice to play music which depends on subtle phrasing for its power, so early instruments are very good for classical and early romantic music, which is the meat and drink of the repertoire."

The recent boom in period instrument concerts and recordings has had a stimulating effect on the established clarinet repertoire, Pay maintains. "It's bringing a fresh look. There are lots of Mozart piano concertos, for example, but only one Mozart Clarinet Concerto, which you quickly become familiar with. So when you come to play it on a different instrument, it's very refreshing: the music is the same but you have different problems, and different solutions. This effect has been very useful for everyone."

With the constant rediscovery of old clarinet pieces, a large existing repertoire, and new approaches to the repertoire being opened up by period instruments, it makes it an exciting time to be a clarinet player or listener.

THE FINEST PERFORMERS

Chosen by Michael Bryant, Vice President of the British Clarinet Society

The senior figure in clarinet playing in this country is Jack Brymer. He's inimitable; no-one plays like he does. He has an incredible list of recordings, both as a soloist and orchestral player. He and his eminent contemporary, Gervase de Peyer, who went to the US and has also made many recordings, are probably the people who have influenced most clarinettists.

The Swiss player Hans Rudolf Stalder was the first to record the Mozart Concerto on basset clarinet – a clarinet with extra low notes – in 1969. He started as an orchestral player, became a soloist, and began to explore the early instruments – the chalumeau, and the boxwood seven- and five-keyed clarinets. He's done some fantastic historical research and pioneering in this field and is leading the exploration into the full range and repertoire of the clarinet.

In Britain Tony Pay is equally important. He's one of the best players in the country in my opinion, who was first clarinettist with the London Sinfonietta and Nash Ensemble. Keith Puddy got a Leverhulme Trust award to explore early performance practice and is an excellent scholar who plays the early instruments as well.

Alan Hacker is another clarinettist who plays

everything. He pioneered the early clarinet and was Professor of Clarinet at the Royal Academy of Music before moving to York University. He's one the best players around; his control of the high notes is an example to all. For example, high C is normally taken to be the highest possible on the instrument. Maxwell Davies's *Hymnos* demands the E above it, played very quietly, but Hacker plays it perfectly.

The film **Out of Africa** starred Robert Redford, Meryl Streep and Mozart's Clarinet Concerto.

THE BEST CD RECORDINGS

Selected by Michael Bryant

Thea King has done an enormous amount of good work with Hyperion. Her CD "The Clarinet in Concert 2" (CDA 66300) has many good lesser-known works on it: the Spohr *Variations*, the Solère *Sinfonietta*, the Rietz Concerto and Heinze's *Konzertstücke*. Rietz helped Mendelssohn in the theatre and in the Bach revival and his work sounds like Mendelssohn at times. Heinze was a composer-clarinettist whose music is reminiscent of Weber – great stuff.

In recent times Dieter Klöcker has done most for the forgotten repertoire, such as on his CD of Quintets by Meyerbeer, Spohr and Bärmann (Orfeo C213901A). He hunted all over Europe for the Meyerbeer and eventually found it in the possession of the descendants of Bärmann, for whom it was written. The *Adagio* of the Bärmann has been recorded many times and was falsely credited to Wagner for a time.

Mozart has got to be in there somewhere, and a CD that's very good value for money is Joy Farrall's playing of the Concerto in A, K622, Trio in E flat, and Clarinet Quintet. Her tone is extremely pleasing on the basset clarinet; you can't wish for better (Meridian CDE84169).

Among modern works, the Corigliano Clarinet Concerto is a phenomenal experience, unlike any other for the instrument. The second movement is an elegy in memory of the composer's father and has great stillness and calmness. There are two versions, by Stanley Drucker (New World NW309-2) and Richard Stoltzman (RCA RD87762), with nothing to choose between them.

Finally, there are lots of good things on the Bayer and Koch labels, some rare. And two things it would be nice to see on CD are Berio's orchestration of the Brahms Clarinet Sonata No. 1, and Colin Matthews's orchestration of the one-movement sketch for a Clarinet Concerto left by Benjamin Britten.

THE OBOE

The most vocal and exotic of the woodwinds

There's something special about the sound of the oboe. It's the most vocal and exotic of the woodwinds, with its double reed giving a peculiarly nasal tone and that *muezzin*-like crack at the beginning of a note. And there's a whole range of oboe sounds too, with widely varying regional twangs and even individual accents – oboists make their own reeds, and hence determine their own personal sound. It's a complex process. A tube of bamboo is split into three or four lengths; the inside is gouged out; that length is scored in the middle and folded over; the result is fitted over a last-like clamp and shaped; then that is tied onto a cork-based brass tube called a staple and scraped off at the top. Different countries scrape different shapes, leading to different sounds. British players tend to leave a U-shaped cross-section, French players a V-shape, and American players a W-shape.

Leon Goossens was the first English oboe player of note and taught many modern players who have gone on to become famous oboists in their own right.

Then the oboist can actually get round to playing the instrument – but again there are different styles. The Viennese oboe retains the ornate baroque-oboe shape and has a metallic sound; most Ameri-can players trad tionally have a shallow sound with a fast vibrato; the Czech style is more flamboyant, freer, and with a wide vibrato. But, as with the English language, the regional accents are being mixed out into a smooth mid-Atlantic sound, as the music business becomes more internationally based. Players are now influenced by several national styles: Paris, for example, the seat of great oboe playing, has a Swiss-German (Heinz Holliger) teaching there. The loss of diversity is mourned by some oboists, but perhaps it's just another consequence of a shrinking world.

The oboe didn't evolve, like most wind instruments: it was virtually invented. Double-reed instruments have been around as long as music itself, and one such group of instruments – the shawm family, some members of which were called 'hautbois' – was a familiar part of outdoor music-making. The only problem with the shawm was its volume: it was far too loud to be played indoors without drowning out other instruments. The story goes that Louis XIV asked the composer Jean-Baptiste Lully and the instrument maker Jean Hotteterre to make an 'indoor shawm' in the mid-seventeenth century, and they came up with the oboe; indeed, many people credit Hotteterre as the inventor of the instrument. The new instrument was very different from the shawm, with engineering that was very sophisticated for the time, and with its sweet tone, agility and ability to play a wide range of dynamics from very soft to loud, it became a popular part of small bands. French courts boasted groups of 16 or 32 players of the oboe or the bassoon, the oboe's double-reeded cousin. Hotteterre's grandson Jacques included an appendix about the new instrument in his seminal flute tutor.

The oboe has a distinctive sound, but a narrow range

Composers were quick to exploit the instrument and particularly its vocal qualities. A Purcell song from *Come, Ye Sons of Art, Away* of 1694 contrasts the soprano's voice against a florid oboe obbligato that imitates the voice. Vivaldi wrote something like two dozen concertos for the oboe in the early 1700s, and Albinoni's concertos call for solo and duo oboes. The great difficulty of some of the writing shows that there must have been some very skilled players around. Handel, who played the oboe himself and often wrote tricky lines for the instrument, wrote for massed oboes and included two solo oboe parts in the "Arrival of the Queen of Sheba" (from the oratorio *Solomon* of 1749) almost making it a double concerto. But probably the composer with the deepest understanding of the instrument in this period was J S Bach; his oboe lines are often very extended and taxing, and they weave around the voice very effectively in the cantatas, masses and and passions. But even Bach's challenging writing is simple compared to the notorious Jan Dismas Zelenka, whose trio sonatas for oboe demand extraordinary virtuosity: strange leaps, very fast runs, and lines so long they can only be played by 'circular breathing': when breathing in, between periods of blowing normally through the instrument, the player takes air in through the nose while forcing air out through the mouth with the cheeks – if done properly this produces a constant stream of air through the instrument and indefinitely long notes.

The baroque period was a heyday for the oboe, and in many ways it was the wind equivalent of the violin. It took a firm place in the orchestra, being used by composers far more than the flute or clarinet, and it is often said that the wind section is built around the oboe. In any case, the oboe's first responsibility in an orchestral piece is to sound the A to which every other instrument tunes up – a task not as easy as it sounds, because the player has to keep a pure and perfectly constant pitch for approximately half a minute or so.

Aranjuez Palace in Spain was the inspiration for Joaquín Rodrigo's Guitar Concerto "Aranjuez", whose famous slow movement features a beautiful melody for the cor anglais.

Mozart, arguably the greatest writer for wind instruments, put several important oboe parts in his serenades, and his Oboe Concerto and Quartet are two of the linchpins of the repertoire. However, the Concerto is the subject of some controversy. We know from Mozart's letters that one Friedrich Ramm played it five times in Mannheim in 1778, and that Mozart transcribed it as a flute concerto to fulfil a commission quickly. The original oboe version, lost for over 150 years, was apparently discovered in Salzburg in 1920, but there are doubts about its authenticity: many suspect the 'rediscovered' manuscript was not written by Mozart.

As with all other instruments, especially the wind instruments, the nineteenth century saw great advances in the construction of the oboe. A maker called Triebert was mainly responsible for the modern oboe, and the shape of the instrument made by his colleague Gillet is the one seen today. The old baroque oboe had a single key, and most notes were made by the player merely covering holes with fingers; the problem with this was that the instrument could only play successfully in a few keys. The improved versions had more complex keywork which enabled any scale to be played convincingly, encouraging the oboe composer to write for a wider range of keys.

Oddly enough, the advances in the oboe seemed merely to have the effect of reducing the amount of solo music written for it; the concerto was the big genre of the romantic movement of the mid- and late-nineteenth century, but the main vehicle was usually the violin or piano, and what oboe music there is tends to be the product of lesser-known names such as Pasculli and Kalliwoda, whose paraphrases of contemporary operas are tackled by every player sometime but seldom heard outside the practice room. The fragment of Beethoven's Oboe Concerto that survives would have been for the classical instrument. Rimsky-Korsakov wrote a set of variations for oboe and wind band, and Schumann three Romances for oboe, but the main work for the oboist was in orchestral playing: Brahms's Violin Concerto includes an eloquent solo, and its dedicatee Joseph Joachim is said to have complained that there was only one tune, and that was given to the oboe. Perhaps the reluctance of composers to use the oboa in concertos was due to its small range – barely more than two octaves – which limits the ability for the 'big statement'.

In this century, Ravel's *Daphnis and Chloë* is notorious for its difficult oboe part (being very high but very quiet) and his *Tombeau de Couperin* suite has a demanding oboe part; he must have been writing for gifted players. Vaughan Williams, Martinu and Richard Strauss all wrote concertos, but there have been very few solo works. Britten's *Six Metapmorphoses After Ovid* is well known, and Luciano Berio's *Sequenza V* for Heinz Holliger displays many contemporary techniques such as chords, flutter-tonguing, and alternative fingerings producing different tone-colours for the same note.

The oboe has three common related instruments: the oboe d'amore, a third lower than the normal oboe and used extensively by Bach; the rarely used bass oboe (used in "Saturn" from Holst's *Planets* Suite to depict the hollow, defeated monologue of an old man); and the cor anglais. Despite its name, this is neither a horn ('cor' in French) nor is it English. It is

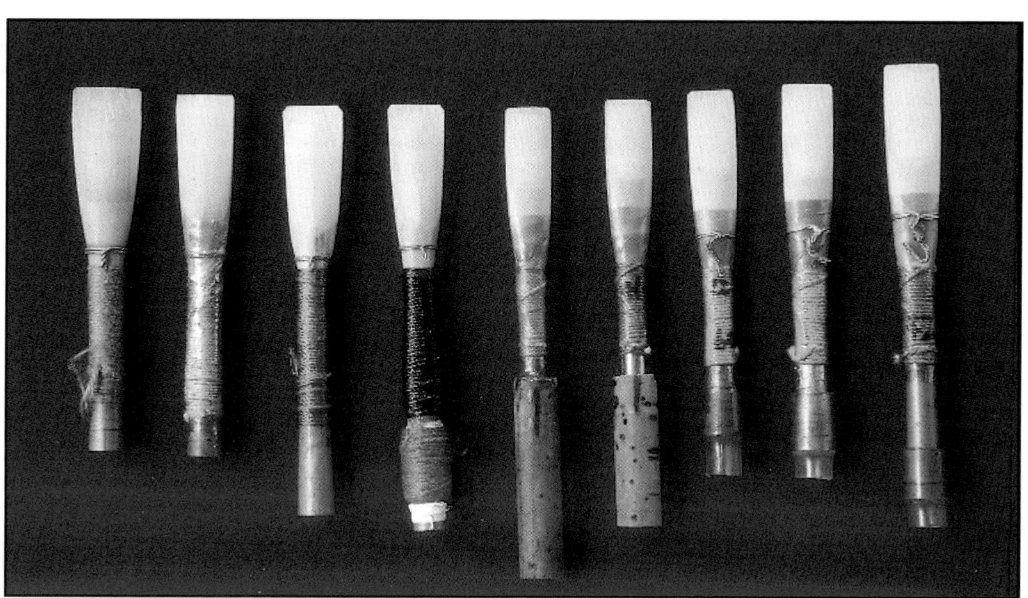

The way an oboe reed is cut determines the sound the instrument produces, and the pattern cut by players varies from country to country, and individual to individual.

Heinz Holliger of Switzerland is one of the foremost players of the oboe in the world today, and his recordings of the standard oboe repertoire are among the very best available.

actually a tenor oboe; the name is often said to come from 'cor anglé' – 'angled horn', from its original dog-leg shape – but there is no real evidence for the idea. Haydn was one of the very earliest composers to use it in a symphony (his *Philosopher* Symphony, No. 22). A familiar modern work that uses the cor anglais is probably Rodrigo's *Concierto de Aranjuez* for guitar. In its famous second movement the melancholy cor anglais seems to imitate a Moorish singer accompanied by the guitar.

The modern oboe has plenty of problems to cope with in addition to finding suitable repertoire. The tiny reed means that plenty of air pressure has to be applied, leading to the clichéd image of the grimacing oboist, and the sensitivity and fragility of reeds obliges players to keep several on the go, keeping some for practice, some for performing Bach, some for performing Stravinsky, and so on. But the oboe's unique and haunting sound surely makes it worthwhile.

THE FINEST PERFORMERS

Selected by oboist Laurence Frankel

The big two are Heinz Holliger of Switzerland and Maurice Bourgue of France. Holliger is very Germanic, totally dedicated, a true professional who practises constantly; Bourgue is more Gallic, laid-back and uninhibited. Despite, or maybe because of, their very different personalities and approach to music, they are great friends and have recorded all the two-oboe repertoire together.

The first English player of note was the celebrated Leon Goossens who taught legions of players currently playing in British orchestras today (such as Neil Black). Another great influence has been Evelyn Rothwell, a great teacher at the Academy until recently, who taught many fine players. She had two concertos (by Pergolesi and Corelli) arranged for her by her husband, Sir John Barbirolli. Other English players worth mentioning are John Anderson, Douglas Boyd, Nick Daniel, David Theodore, Derek Wickens and Gordon Hunt. Paul Goodwin, who plays with the English Concert, is becoming quite well known and has made some good recordings on the period oboe.

Outside Britain, Jürg Schaeftlein taught many players of the baroque and classical oboe. Ray Still shows the American oboe style, and has played in baroque quartets with Perlman and Zukerman, while Gerhard Turetschek exemplifies the Vienna Philharmonic style. Lothar Koch, principal of the Berlin Philharmonic Orchestra, was succeeded by Hansjörg Schellenberger, who is now recording all the major repertoire and is a good name to watch out for.

"Cor anglais" means "English horn" – but it is neither a horn nor English.

THE BEST CD RECORDINGS

Chosen by Laurence Frankel

The recordings of the oboist Heinz Holliger are a must, and those on Philips of Vivaldi Concertos show off some of his finest and most sublime playing (432 059-2). He is joined by the equally essential Maurice Bourgue on a set of sonatas for two oboes, bassoon and continuo by Zelenka that shows the peaks of virtuosity that must have existed at a time when the oboe was still developing (Archiv 423 937-2).

The Mozart Oboe Concerto is a linchpin of the repertoire, and a very satisfying performance is by Douglas Boyd on ASV (CDCOE808) – the orchestra is first-rate too. It comes coupled with the Richard Strauss Oboe Concerto.

Finally, a vintage recording of the oboe in a chamber setting is Vladimir Ashkenazy and the London Wind Soloists in a disc of Mozart and Beethoven wind quintets on Decca. Terence McDonagh is the oboist (421 151-2).

THE BASSOON
The orchestral clown

If you asked a Martian to design an instrument, they'd probably come up with something like the bassoon. The layout of keys defies logical analysis, resembles that of no other wind instrument, and makes it infernally difficult to play. It isn't even clear to the beginner how to fit the parts together when you take it out of the case. And there is something distinctly odd about an instrument that appears to be aimed bazooka-like towards passing aircraft instead of at the audience. The bassoon's image isn't helped by its now automatic use in film and television soundtracks to accompany old or bumbling or plain comical characters – something Prokofiev did in his *Peter and the Wolf* to go with the grumpy grandfather in the children's story – which has contributed to its unfair tag of the 'clown of the orchestra'.

But the bassoon is far more than that. It has a range of three-and-a-half octaves, covering the bass, tenor, and some of the soprano register; down at the bottom it has that rich, sonorous sound ("dark red velvet and velvet-black", as composer Andrzej Panufnik described it when writing his recent Concerto) while at the top its tone is expressive and plaintive, as demonstrated in the first bars of Stravinsky's *Rite of Spring*. The bassoon solo that opens this work starts in the very top, very difficult part of the instrument's range – going from high C to high D – and is clearly meant to give a feeling of strain and effort. Continually rising standards have meant that modern orchestral bassoonists can manage the notes rather more easily than their predecessors, leading some critics to suggest half-jokingly that the opening phrase should be transposed upwards a semitone every few years to preserve Stravinsky's original intentions.

The keywork of the **bassoon** is very complicated, and makes producing even a simple scale involve a very tricky sequence of finger movements.

"In that the tone is personal, vocal, and lyrical," says the bassoonist Daniel Smith, "it's the wind equivalent of the cello. You can personalise your playing to a great extent, but to get there you have to serve a long, hard apprenticeship." He points to the extraordinary technical problems facing the learner:

A high-quality modern bassoon can cost the same as a family car.

the thumb of the left hand can play the keys around it in ten different ways, for example, and the thumb of the right hand four ways. It makes even a simple run up a scale involve many complex changes of fingering.

But the technical challenges to the player of the modern keyed instrument are nothing compared to those which faced the bassoonist of Vivaldi's time. The bassoon was a relatively new instrument in the early eighteenth century. It was like its predecessor, the dulcian, in that it was a hairpin-shaped wind instrument; but unlike the dulcian it was now being made in three sections bundled together – hence the Italian word for bassoon, fagotto, which is related to the English word "faggot" meaning "bundle of sticks". The jointed bassoon, which had appeared in France in the seventeenth century, presented fewer problems of construction and could be made longer and lighter than before, enabling the upper register to be extended and developed.

The number of keys on a bassoon increased over the years to enable players to make more notes that fingers simply couldn't reach on the huge instrument. One made by Denner of Nuremberg around 1700 had three; that of Stanesby of London from 1747 had four; Kirst of Potsdam made one around 1800 with seven; by the mid nineteenth century, the techniques of engineer and instrument maker Theobald Boehm (1793–1881) had been applied to make bassoons with 30 keys – and the consequent range of complicated fingerings needed to control them all. The Rolls-Royce of modern bassoons is that made by Heckel, which can cost more than a luxury family car.

If the keywork has changed, the basic method of sound production has not. Most wind instruments, such as a clarinet, use a single reed; on a bassoon, as with the oboe, the player blows between two reeds that are fixed together and vibrate against each other. It is this double-reed that gives the bassoon its characteristic sound quality – but the extra depth comes at a cost. Double reeds are notoriously short-lived and inconsistent in quality, "which has a very important effect on the sound," says Smith. "If it's not responsive, you have to compromise." He reckons to get only a few days of recording-quality use from any one reed, and keeps lists of reeds labelled A to Z so that he can always use one of a condition appropriate to the playing situation – recording, minor concert, practice and so on. When you are involved in projects such as recording Vivaldi's several dozen bassoon concertos – as Smith has been – such planning is vital.

Vivaldi wrote nearly 40 concertos which are generally thought to be for the bassoon. If so they are among the earliest masterpieces for the instrument, and Smith raves about them all (he has recorded them on ASV, available as a set or in six volumes). "All but one is in three movements," he says, "fast-slow-fast, with great excitement in the outer movements and

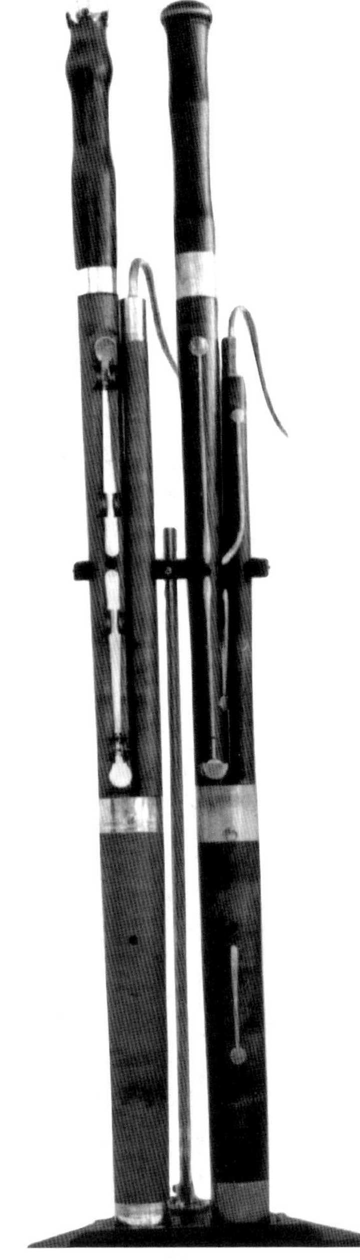

The bassoons built in **Vivaldi's** time lacked the keywork of modern instruments, making them even more difficult to play

breathtaking lyrical beauty in the inner." They present formidable technical problems even to the modern player, and must have been even more of a challenge on the older style of bassoon with only a few keys. Many, says Smith, were played by young ladies at the Ospedale della Pietà in Venice, a charitable institution for foundling girls where Vivaldi was in charge of musical education. "I just don't know how they could play them," admits Smith, "they are harder than Mozart. There must have been some extraordinary musicians among them. Playing Vivaldi is a great way to improve your technique."

The rich bass properties of the bassoon made it an essential part of the orchestra from early on, even if it did not always have an independent line but merely doubled the bass-line elsewhere. The Bachs, Telemann, Mozart and their contemporaries all included it in their orchestral writing. The second Bourée of J S Bach's Orchestral Suite No. 4 requires some virtuosic fluency in a difficult key, indicating that there must have been some excellent players of the bassoon. English orchestras had become so fond of the bassoon and the double-bassoon, which was an octave lower, that they became the target for the satirists: the *General Advertiser* of 20 October 1740 had a spoof concert listing for "a concerto of twenty-four Bassoons accompanied on the violoncello, intermixed with duets by four double bassoons…"

The bassoon has spawned many solo works, though few as good as the Concerto by Mozart of 1774. It shows how thoroughly he understood the nature and potential of the bassoon, as he did all wind instruments. There are plenty of other solo and orchestral bassoon works by the likes of Kozeluch, Danzi, Vanhal, Hummel and Berwald, while Weber's Concerto of 1820 and *Andante and Hungarian Rondo* are standard concert pieces even today. Other smaller-scale works involving the bassoon include the *Symphonias concertante* by Mozart and Haydn, and Paganini's *Concertante* for bassoon and horn.

In the twentieth century the repertoire has been boosted by works for bassoon and orchestra from Villa-Lobos, Gordon Jacob and Elizabeth Maconchy, with concertante works from Richard Strauss and Hindemith, plus sonatas by Saint-Saëns, Dutilleux and Tansman. Claude Bolling wrote a jazz suite for the instrument, but its use in

Kim Walker is one of Britain's up-and-coming young bassoonists.

jazz has been limited, possibly because of its technical difficulties; Daniel Smith, a keen jazzman, has only seen it used this way by one group – a 1950s outfit, the Australian Jazz Quintet.

The instrument has not yet had a face popularly associated with it: there is no bassoon equivalent of James Galway, Andrés Segovia or Dennis Brain. But, thinks Daniel Smith, this could be about to change. "We're still establishing the sound of the bassoon," he says, "which is a fascinating process above and beyond the music. People don't appreciate the repertoire and range of the instrument," he says. "When they hear one of my recitals, they are astonished. "To prove the bassoon can be

The novel version of Prokofiev's **Peter and the Wolf** recorded by Deutsche Grammophon...

popular he has recorded a CD of "Bassoon Bon-Bons", arrangements of popular tunes such as Chopin études, Schubert serenades and opera arias such as Verdi's "La donna è mobile" that show off the lyrical side of the instrument.

Smith is confident that the bassoon will be the next instrument to become popular, and when he meets resistance from concert managers who are not usually convinced that a bassoon recital will bring in the crowds, he points to passages from the flautist Jean-Pierre Rampal's autobiography that give the identical misgivings of 1950s concert managers; shortly afterwards, of course, the flute took off, and Smith believes the same will happen to the bassoon. "It's overdue for a boom," he says. "It's the next one that's going to happen."

THE FINEST PERFORMERS

Chosen by bassoon virtuoso Daniel Smith

The great pioneer was the British player Archie Camden, who helped popularise the instrument. When he played the first notes of *The Rite of Spring* everyone was astonished. Of course, every conservatory player can manage that now, but at the time it was like the four-minute mile. He also was the first to record the Mozart Concerto and did it incredibly well.

Gwydion Brooke also recorded a Mozart concerto – a

...illustrated the cliché image of the "grumpy bassoon" which goes with the grandfather character.

transcription of a violin concerto – and is another important name.

The Yugoslav player Milan Turkovich has recorded a lot of music on Deutsche Grammophon and is a brilliant player with a clear technique, and the Frenchman Maurice Alard is another splendid player worth picking out.

Klaus Thunemann has a very personal style. He makes the instrument sing, and he makes it come alive. He's certainly different; I love his sound. Finally, a good young British player, Kim Walker, is worth watching.

THE BEST CD RECORDINGS

Selected by Nick Ingamells of the Double Reed Society

Perhaps the most sympathetic environment for the bassoon is not the solo platform but the orchestra or chamber ensemble. Some of the finest writing for the instrument may be found in Mozart's piano concertos, and late symphonies; Respighi's *Three Botticelli Pictures*; Rimsky-Korsakov's *Scheherazade*; and Stravinsky's *The Soldier's Tale*.

The Archiv recording of Zelenka's Six Trio Sonatas (Archiv 423 937-2) – a classic combination of Thunemann with oboists Heinz Holliger and Maurice Bourgue – is too good to miss. These sonatas were conceived on a grand scale, with remarkable harmonic twists and bold instrumentation that elevates the bassoon from mere continuo to virtual solo status. Dombrecht, Ponseele and Danny Bond (Accent ACC8848D) provide an interesting comparison on period instruments.

The wind soloists of the Chamber Orchestra of Europe have made many fine recordings in recent years, and one of the most interesting is a selection of works by Dvorak, Janacek, Hummel, Seiber and Krommer, with exciting and accomplished bassoon playing from Matthew Wilkie and Christopher Gunia (ASV CDCOE812).

No collection would complete without an example of the lyrical French bassoon, demonstrated with typically Gallic flair by Amaury Wallacz, Pascal Rogé and friends in Poulenc's Trio and Sextet (Decca 421 581-2). Both pieces draw heavily on the performers' technical and emotional reserves, and in this recording all present rise to the occasion with style and grace.

THE FRENCH HORN

Thirty feet of precision engineering

Of all the instruments in the orchestra, the French horn is accepted as the most difficult to play. The amount of technique and practice needed can't be overestimated. Lip pressure is so critical that split notes, the ones either side of where they should be, are very difficult to avoid. It is tiring on the lungs too: you'll occasionally see three horn players in an orchestra playing two parts, with one player, called a 'bumper', taking the simpler lines after a soloist has played their obbligato so they can get their breath back.

A conch shell doesn't sound an ideal tool with which to tackle one of the Mozart Horn Concertos but, in essence, that's what a horn is: a small-mouthpieced, conical tube that developed into a 30-foot metal spaghetti of precision engineering, which actually does sound musical – if it's played well. Dennis Brain, perhaps the greatest horn player that ever drew breath – and then so perfectly expelled it – said things were simple. To get the right lip position or embouchure, just smile, he said, and then imagine pushing a hair off your tongue with your lips. He had such control he could even get a tune out of a hosepipe; to prove the point he once did just that at the Royal Albert Hall, playing the Leopold Mozart Alpine Horn Concerto on a length of green garden hose fitted with a mouthpiece.

The horn of Bach and Handel's time was a rather different instrument from the valved machine of today (but just as un-Gallic: there's nothing particularly French about the instrument). As with the hunting horn, the player produced different notes by lip pressure alone just like Brain did with the hose. Bach's first *Brandenburg Concerto* features a horn, and his Bach B minor Mass has a horn obbligato, but it was seen as an accompanying rather than solo instrument. This didn't stop a contemporary of Bach's, Jan Dismas Zelenka, from writing some phenomenally difficult horn music which is being revived today.

Mozart's four horn concertos remain unsurpassed masterpieces for the instrument after over 200 years.

The notes demanded by Bach and Handel were mainly from the 'harmonic series', the notes obtained purely by altering the shape of the lips and the air pressure. However, players had begun to realise the curious effect of sticking their hand up the bell. In some positions the notes could be altered slightly up or down, filling out the gaps in the horn's range. This 'hand-stopping' is used to some extent in the *Brandenburgs*, but a player called Hampel in the 1730s and 1740s refined the techniques to prove that a horn really could play enough notes to let it tackle lyrical and tuneful music.

The **French horn** demands high-precision engineering to make – and high-precision playing.

Music for the solo horn took off to the extent that concertos began to appear. Vivaldi wrote two for two horns, and Mozart produced four masterpieces in the 1780s. They were written for a friend of his, Leutgeb, and are full of musical and personal in-jokes. The scores are written in a bewildering range of coloured inks to put the player off, are peppered with insults ("bet you can't play this bit, you donkey" and similar) and even include deliberate mistakes to make members of the audience not in on the joke think the horn player messed up. At one point a phrase is played twice, as if the soloist came in too early the first time.

The horn features in another of Mozart's tongue-in-cheek pieces. *Ein musikalischer Späß* (usually translated as "A Musical Joke") gently pokes fun at second-division composers and enthusiastic but inexpert eighteenth-century village bands. There are deliberately clumsy sequences of notes that sound totally out of tune or comically muffled. The last movement is familiar as the theme tune to *The Horse of the Year Show*, but doesn't sound funny at all to modern ears, apart perhaps from its chaotic ending in a series of nonsense chords.

At the beginning of the nineteenth century Beethoven wrote solos for the horn in the third movements of his Third and Eighth Symphonies. He was the major force behind the revolution that took music from the classical to the romantic era – a similar revolution was about to change the sound and character of the French horn. In the 1840s, reliability of engineering techniques had improved to the point where valves could be safely added. This evened out the

The smooth curves of the **natural horn** show the simplicity of the instrument – no valves! Different notes have to be produced purely by the player altering the air pressure.

muffled and dampened sounds of the hand-stopped natural horn and widened the range of possible notes, so that the new instrument was no longer restricted to one key per piece. Composers such as Schumann, Wagner, Brahms and Tchaikovsky wrote for the improved instrument. The big, round romantic sound could be carried well by the new horn with its ability to carry a chromatic, non-martial tune.

Schumann's *Konzertstück* is an excellent example of the new writing. It is intended for two natural and two valve horns, while Brahms's Trio for horn, violin and piano, written just after his mother died, is arguably the best romantic horn piece.

Despite the advances offered by the valve technology, the horn was still an unfashionable instrument up to the middle of the twentieth century, with relatively little written for it. Essentially, it was just too hard to play; composing a concerto was a waste of time because half the notes would inevitably be split by the struggling player.

Or so it was thought, until Dennis Brain, a young Englishman, transformed horn music in the middle of this century. Through his incredible technique he showed the instrument could be mastered and gave it respectability; Richard Strauss and Paul Hindemith wrote concertos, and at last the horn had arrived. But this sparkling career was to be tragically cut short. At 6am on 1 September 1957 the 36-year-old Brain, driving his open-top sports car back from the Edinburgh Festival in driving rain, crashed into an elm tree in Hertfordshire and died instantly. Poulenc's *Elegy* for horn and piano, written subsequently, includes a section depicting the crash. Such was the admiration commanded by Brain that his horn, crumpled like a newspaper in the accident, was restored after months of work by the London horn makers Paxman.

"It was a labour of love," says head of the company Bob Paxman, "with several people working on different sections. In the same time we could have built two new horns, but the restoration was done for sentimental reasons, at the request of his family."

Building a new horn isn't an easy job either. "There's an immense amount of handicraft work. The rotary valves have to very precisely fitted into their cases, with exactly three quarters of a thousandth of an inch clearance round the valves – loose enough to rotate, but tight enough to be airtight," says Paxman. The horn is not therefore a cheap instrument: an inexpensive Italian-made 'starter' horn costs around £1,000, with a good professional-quality triple horn – one pitched to play in three different keys – anything up to £3,300.

This is obviously a disincentive to the young musician. And, with no jazz or pop stimulus such as that enjoyed by the saxophone, flute or trumpet, the horn seems to offer little to aspiring wind players. Even Glenn Miller's band never used a French horn. All this makes the horn rather unfashionable these days, even though there are more players than ever before.

But the horn repertoire is being swelled all the time by leading British composers such as Sir Malcolm Arnold, Alun Hoddinott, Sir Peter Maxwell Davies, and Michael Berkeley. "There is quite a lot of music being written for the horn," says Berkeley, "and certainly horn music is in the front of most contemporary composers' minds. It's a wonderful instrument and the orchestra would be a very poor place without it."

There still isn't much incentive to write concertos, however; concerts rarely feature horn concertos and this, combined with the difficulty of finding soloists, makes it a "slightly perilous exercise", according to Berkeley. His as yet unrecorded Concerto was written for Michael Thompson and premièred at the Cheltenham Festival in 1984.

When writing for players of Thompson's astounding ability, technique presents no problems. "Michael is wonderful. Players like him ask you to write the music you want to hear, and then they try to play it," says Berkeley. He and Thompson tried out the sketches of the work as it was being composed to test which phrases worked best: "I find I tend to write too high for the horn," he says, "and though the player can manage, some ways in which you approach the high notes sound better than others. Some ways sound like you're running up the hill, others as if you've jumped effortlessly".

But essentially these technical aspects of composition hold few problems for the professional. "To a certain extent it's just experience, knowing

Dennis Brain was in many people's minds the greatest horn player of this, and possibly of any, century. His career was tragically cut short by a fatal car accident.

what will work, and obviously you study a lot of scores, and listen to a lot of horn music. For a composer, instruments like the guitar and harp are more difficult to write for than the horn. The horn is at the centre of things, and as a child I was shown by my father how the horn holds harmony together." Berkeley had a useful father for a future composer – Sir Lennox Berkeley, a major composer himself. His Horn Trio, along with the Strauss Horn Concertos and the Britten *Serenade*, were among the works the younger Berkeley listened to in preparation for writing the Concerto.

"I also looked at Peter Maxwell Davies's music – he gets some extraordinary sounds from the use of harmonics, and I found that interesting." The technique of harmonics – singing a note while playing another, which by a phenomenon of physics produces four-note chords – is one of the more curious effects that can be obtained on the instrument.

Berkeley can see no pros-pect of the old natural valveless horn making its way into modern music, despite a revival of interest in authentic instruments. "I can't see much point writing for the hand horn. The valve horn offers twentieth-century music much more, with its chromatic possibilities. For early music it's fine, but there are no advantages for the modern composer."

Nevertheless, the interest in authentic instruments that swept through the 1980s has had a remarkable effect on horn music. Suddenly the old natural horn is back in fashion, and pre-valve horn works such as the Mozart Concertos are being recorded and played on the instruments they were written for by players such as Anthony Halstead and Hermann Baumann.

As with many other instruments in the authentic music debate, there is a lively and ongoing argument about whether the coarse and earthy sound of the old horn is preferable to the smoother and more sophisticated modern instrument for music of that period. Is playing music on the natural horn in the 1990s one step forward, or two steps back? Horn player and reviewer Stuart Nickless is an enthusiast of the natural instrument. "The range of sounds you hear on the natural horn sounds uneven compared with the constant tone of the valve horn: some

Dennis Brain proving that a player as talented as him could get a tune out of a hosepipe – by playing the Leopold Mozart Alpine Horn Concerto on a length of standard garden hose at a Hoffnung Festival Concert on 13 November 1956.

notes come out bright and crisp, some muffled and blurred. And composers wrote for that sound. They knew what it would produce: it's limited, but richer. You get much more depth of tone-colour, and people like Mozart knew how to use that effectively."

"Several horn players think the natural sound is irritating and ugly, with no purity, but I think that when you play music written for the natural horn on a valve horn you lose a lot of nuances the composer intended. Of course, you have the same debate across the whole authentic field. When you look at the phenomenally difficult horn parts in, say, Haydn's *Sturm und Drang* period, you realise that he was writing for exceptionally good players. Fortunately today's players have re-learnt old techniques and done very well.

"The explosion of interest in the natural horn has been great. It's given it a whole new lease of life, and has added dimensions to the instrument."

Paradoxically, perhaps the French horn's future lies in rediscovering its past.

The Finest Performers

Selected by horn player Stuart Nickless

You can't underestimate the influence of Dennis Brain on horn music. He made the horn into a solo as well as orchestral instrument, through his incredible musicianship, technique and personality. He basically showed composers that it was an instrument worth writing for. And his 1954 recordings of the Mozart Horn Concertos are still selling today.

After him there was Barry Tuckwell who for a while led the London Symphony Orchestra. Like Brain, he was an out-and-out soloist who mastered the instrument. He established himself as probably the leading player of the 1970s and early 1980s, before a new generation of players came along.

Hermann Baumann, his German equivalent, made the first recording of the horn concertos on a natural horn in the early 1970s. He's also got a fabulous technique and musicianship.

Someone who isn't remembered as a soloist is Alan Civil who stayed with the BBC Symphony Orchestra until his death in 1989, and was a great orchestral player. He took over from Brain in the Philharmonia the day after Brain died, which is quite an achievement.

Of the current players two stand out. There's Michael Thompson who was principal of the BBC Scottish Symphony Orchestra at 19. He's a phenomenal player and a superb musician, and currently Professor of the Horn at the Royal Academy. If I reach for a record, it's usually for a Thompson recording.

Finally there's Anthony Halstead the Professor of the Horn at the Guildhall School of Music, who's probably the leading natural horn player at the moment. He's got complete mastery of his instrument and fantastic musicianship – listen to him doing lip trills up a scale! He makes the impossible sound effortless and musical as well. He recorded Weber's *Concertino* for horn and orchestra at short notice on the natural horn, and plays it marvellously.

The Best CD Recordings

Chosen by Stuart Nickless

A good example of the early use of the horn is in Bach's First *Brandenburg Concerto.* There's a good natural horn recording by Anthony Halstead on Archiv (410 500-2), and a modern instrument version is by Timothy Brown under Neville Marriner on Philips (400 076/7-2).

The Mozart Horn Concertos are definitely ones to have. Apart from every tune being familiar, they're lovely pieces, lyrical and tuneful. They show off the more melodic side and the last movement of each one, always in 6/8, harks back to the hunting-horn ancestry of the instrument. Dennis Brain did a recording on EMI (CDH7

61013-2). For the natural horn, Anthony Halstead again on Nimbus (NI5104).

The Schumann *Konzertstück* is a great piece, written for two valve and two natural horns, but always recorded on four valve horns. Three movements use the full range of the horn to give 25 minutes of exciting music, and the sound of the four horns together is brilliant. The recording with the Berlin Phil Horn Quartet is the best one (Koch Schwann 311021).

You often get the two Richard Strauss Horn Concertos on the same CD. He wrote the First when he was 19, and that's another with a hunting-horn 6/8 finale. The Second he wrote at 43, and it's the most taxing of all in terms of length, breadth, difficulty and stamina. Great stuff, melodic and romantic. Again, Dennis Brain on EMI (CDC7 47834-2).

Barry Tuckwell of Australia is one of the most celebrated modern players of the horn.

A very intimate piece is the Brahms Horn Trio for horn, violin and piano. It shows the horn off in a chamber light. It has its dark moods but ends with a positive finale, which is yet another 6/8 hunting-horn piece. Dennis Brain did a live recording at the Edinburgh Festival for the BBC; a natural horn version is now available which is very good (Harmonia Mundi HMU90 7037).

Of modern pieces the best known, and the best piece that was written for Brain, is probably Britten's *Serenade* for tenor, horn and strings. There are several good recordings and any of the players mentioned here do it well (Barry Tuckwell is on Decca 436 395-2, with Peter Pears and Benjamin Britten).

THE TRUMPET

Brash and extrovert with nothing to play?

"People said I was crazy to take up the trumpet seriously because there was no solo repertoire to choose from", says Håkan Hardenberger, who has probably done more than any other trumpeter to change things. It's actually truer to say that there's a yawning gap of some 200 years from the beautiful concertos by Hummel and Haydn to the middle of the twentieth century when Sir Peter Maxwell Davies and Sir Harrison Birtwistle again wrote concertos for the instrument.

The instrument Mozart's father, Leopold, and Haydn's brother Michael, wrote concertos for in the second half of the eighteenth century was very different from the modern valve trumpet. For a start, it had none of the complicated ironmongery and piston valves that make life so much easier for today's players; it consisted of a long brass cylinder, coiled like a garden hose, with a mouthpiece at one end and a bell-shaped opening at the other. Different notes were produced purely by altering the lips and the air pressure.

The sounds produced by this natural trumpet were pretty rough and ready and certainly didn't cover all the notes on the piano keyboard, but were fine for fanfares or sounding the alarm in battle – in fact the tradition of an elite trumpet corps stretches back to the Middle Ages. Throughout Europe trumpeters had become a powerful, organised body of musicians employed directly by the king as a symbol of his own importance and also to entertain the court.

Other musicians, however, were reluctant to let trumpeters join their string-based ensembles because their playing was liable either to drown them out or not be in tune. So instrument-makers set about improving the trumpet: they pitched it in different keys (most commonly D or E flat in Germany and England) and gave it a shallower mouthpiece which made it easier for the player to reach the higher notes. When in the seventeenth century some trumpeters became exempt from their fanfare-playing duties, a much softer style of playing known as clarino developed which was pitched quite high and contained some delicate tone-colours that were achieved by changing the shape of the mouth. The Michael Haydn and Leopold Mozart concertos are among the finest examples of this clarino playing.

By the end of the eighteenth century when Michael Haydn's more famous brother and Johann Hummel were writing trumpet concertos, instrument makers had been trying to make it possible to play the full range of notes on the trumpet. The result was the key trumpet – not a model destined to last.

The traditional role of the trumpet has been that of producing fanfares – one which hasn't inspired composers to write for the solo instrument until recently.

"The key trumpet is an awful instrument," says Hardenberger, who has recorded the Haydn and Hummel concertos but would not dream of playing them on an authentic instrument. "I can see why it didn't survive. The keys are like a saxophone's; you get an incredibly uneven sound. The trumpet is one of the instruments that has developed the most, and it would be horrible to go back to a thing like that. Life is difficult enough without it!"

The smoother sounds of the trumpet we know today, with its valves to cut in or cut out extra lengths of tubing to raise or lower notes and thus fill out those notes that a simple tube couldn't get, are more to Hardenberger's liking. The valve trumpet was significantly improved and updated during the Romantic period: the B flat trumpet took over from the long F trumpet as standard (and still is today, followed by the C trumpet) with its three valves, from which it is possible to play seven different harmonic series. Not that this was much comfort to trumpet soloists, who had virtually no new repertoire coming out in the nineteenth century. Writing for the trumpet was confined to the orchestral parts in a Berlioz overture or a Rossini opera.

The twentieth century hasn't seen an explosion of new repertoire either, but Hardenberger is working on it, commissioning contemporary compo-sers to write for him. He has already recorded highly distinctive concertos by Birtwistle, Maxwell Davies and Michael Blake Watkins on Philips; Hans Werner Henze has also

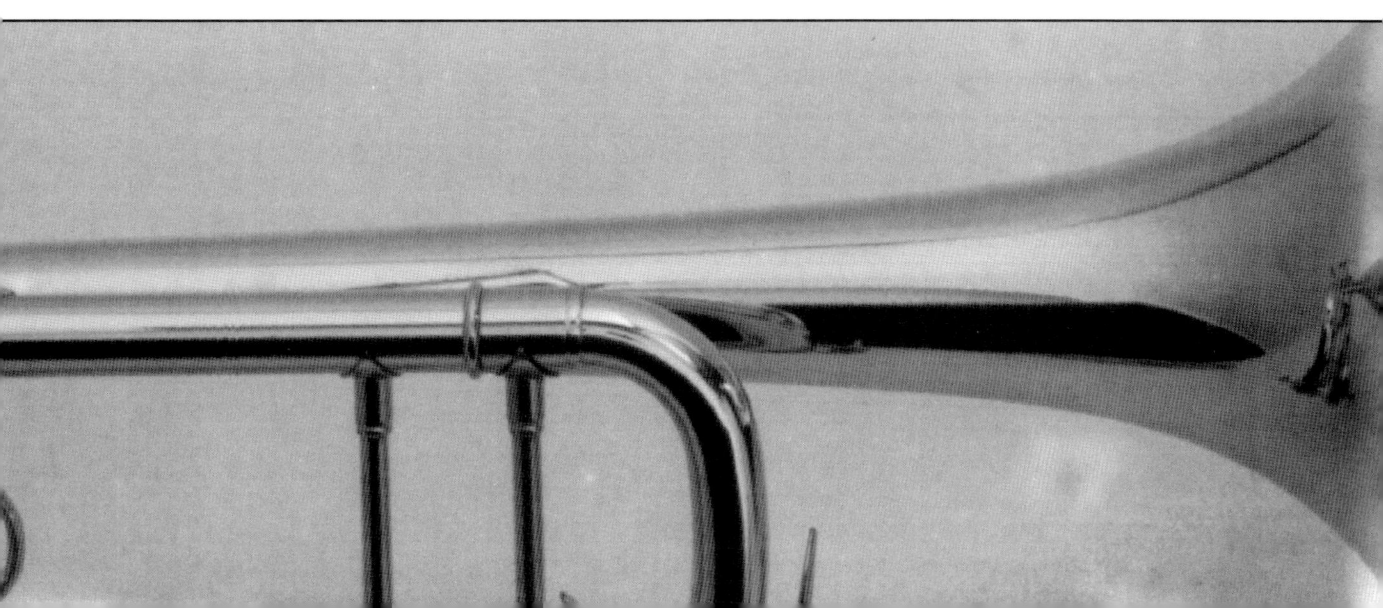

Wynton Marsalis is not only a respected classical trumpet player – he is also a consummate jazzman whose group had the accolade of being asked to play at the 1993 Prom concerts.

written solo music for him. Next on his commissions list is the Japanese composer Toru Takemitsu.

Playing a work no-one else has played before is always difficult, and when the musical language is a challenging one as well, that can push a player very hard. "The Birtwistle was terribly hard, but that's as it should be," he says. "It really pushes the human being and the instrument, with the different colours required, and that's very interesting."

The popularisation of jazz after the Second World War saw the trumpet make its way into the jazz ensemble as an ideal lead instrument with qualities appropriate for the style of music – brash, agile, raunchy, and loud enough to cut across the densest night-club atmosphere; but also polished and refined when the circumstances required. From Louis Armstrong to Miles Davis a succession of trumpeters showed what the instrument could do in that context, while classical soloists were still few in number. One recent player to straddle both worlds, however, is Wynton Marsalis, a highly gifted American trumpeter, who manages to play baroque music on one night and jazz the next – as he showed in 1993 when his jazz band had the accolade of being asked to play at the London Prom Concerts.

Knowledge of jazz's vocabulary and its techniques are vital even for classical trumpeters who don't play jazz, Hardenberger believes. Many of the effects used by jazz players, such as singing one note and playing another to produce the effect of a chord, have been increasingly taken up by classical composers and players. Jazz trumpeters have also pushed the instrument to its highest limits and beyond – though high trumpet parts are more usually tackled by classical players on a piccolo trumpet to save strain on their lips. (The piccolo trumpet is familiar from an unlikely source: it is used in the instrumental break in the middle of the Beatles song *Penny Lane*, and Paul McCartney – who wrote the notes used in the break – was said to have wanted that sound after hearing the piccolo trumpet used in the second of Bach's *Brandenburg Concertos*.)

It's a reminder of the sheer wear and tear involved in playing the instruments. "Playing the trumpet is a physical thing," he says. "You can leave it for two days but you'll have to pay for it afterwards. If I take a week off I need two weeks out of

Håkan Hardenberger is probably the foremost trumpet player of today, who has done a lot to extend the modern repertoire by encouraging composers to write works for him.

concerts just to get back into shape. Such tiny muscles are involved in the mouth, tongue and lips which need to be both strong and flexible. After only two or three days off they get weaker and you lose the muscular memory of the things you've practised." Because of the way delicate muscular tissue in the lips is said to change around the age of 60, trumpeters rarely last beyond their fifties. But Hardenberger isn't daunted and thinks the future for his instruments is bright. "A lot of other instruments have played out their role and are becoming dusty. The quality of the trumpet is that it's new ground, and that's creative."

THE FINEST PERFORMERS

Selected by Håkan Hardenberger

I'd have to pick the jazz trumpeters Miles Davis and Clifford Brown; then Maurice André, the French classical trumpeter. Then I have to pick out Adolph Herseth, who's still playing first trumpet wonderfully in the Chicago Symphony Orchestra in his early seventies, his playing is very correct and it will be interesting to see how long he can go on for.

And then, of course, there's Wynton Marsalis, who has made his name in both the jazz and classical worlds.

THE BEST CD RECORDINGS

Chosen by Hakan Hardenberger

I am a great fan of all that baroque repertoire – the Michael Haydn Concerto is scored with two flutes and strings in a very delicate way. André has a disc of trumpet concertos by Telemann, Michael Haydn and Joseph Haydn (Deutsche Grammophon 419 874-2).

I would also choose Wynton Marsalis playing the Hummel and Haydn concertos with Raymond Leppard and the National Philharmonic on Sony (CD37846) as a must, as well as his disc of baroque duets with the soprano Kathleen Battle (Sony CD46672).

THE TROMBONE

One of the orchestra's most extrovert instruments

"You don't choose to play the trombone," says Simon Hogg, the trombonist with the Fine Arts Brass Ensemble. "It chooses you. It's a loud, extrovert instrument, that makes everyone sit up and take notice."

Trombone players are not known as shy, retiring types. But the instrument is bound to attract people who enjoy their social life: the trombone embraces all eras of music from pre-renaissance to avant-garde, all genres from chamber to symphonic music, and the width of the musical spectrum from straight-laced classical to hot and cool jazz.

The instrument's facility to do a perfect sliding glissando up or down over six semitones is one of its most exploited features. Shostakovich used it to explicit effect at the end of a love scene in his opera *Lady Macbeth of Mtsensk*, for instance (a fact which didn't endear him to Stalin) and many listeners' first impressions of the instrument must be one of bumptious music-hall parping. With enduring clichés like that around, it's no surprise that trombone players don't take themselves too seriously.

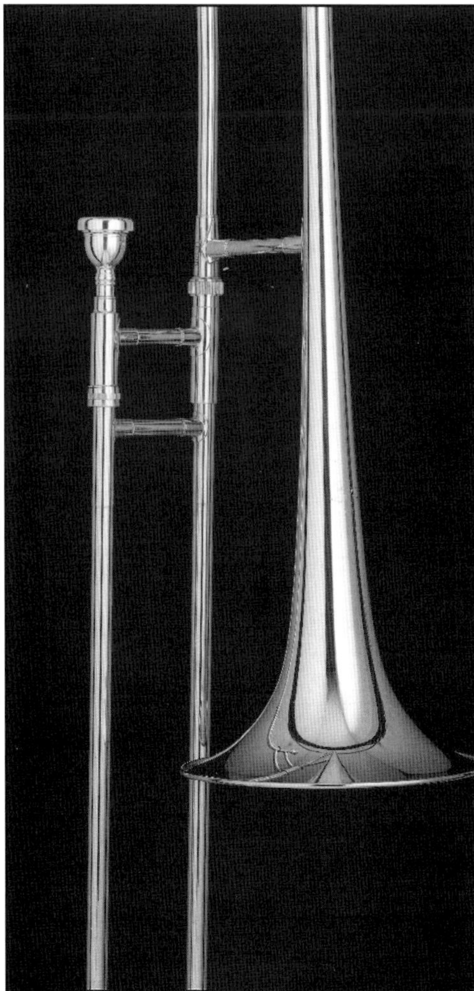

Though its use in jazz makes it seem a 'modern' instrument, the trombone has remained virtually unchanged for hundreds of years.

It's an image that would have been unthinkable four hundred years ago. The trombone had far loftier associations from its widespread and almost exclusive use in church music. A painting of three angels by Filippino Lippi from 1490 in the church of Santa Maria sopra Minerva in Rome shows this. One is playing a dulcimer, one a pipe, and the other – rather comically to modern eyes – appears to be blowing a jazzy trombone solo.

The trombone was for a long time considered the instrument of the Last Trump: a trombone blast would be the divine signal for the Last Judgement. Mozart's last work, his incomplete Requiem, has a symbolic trombone solo for this reason at the beginning of "Tuba mirum". In fact, the trombone was an instrument of such gravity that Mozart used it only in his sacred works and operas. There is a particularly dramatic use of it in the supper scene of *Don Giovanni*, the first time it was ever used in a theatre situation of that kind; the trombone didn't join the orchestra until the late eighteenth century. In 1805 Beethoven, ever an innovator, used trombones to great effect in the final movement of his Fifth Symphony, and his symphonic successor Brahms was an excellent writer for the instrument.

Gradually the trombone moved from small ensembles into military bands, particularly in Germany, where it took on a role of strengthening the bass-line. During the nineteenth century romantic composers found that the trombone could be a versatile instrument capable of expressing a range of emotion, from "religious accent, calm and imposing... to wild clamours of the orgy" as Berlioz put it. The potential for loud playing, so useful in military bands, was used more and more (one bandleader in 1850 made his trombonists play specially designed instruments that had the bell pointing backwards over the shoulder to stop them playing too loudly). The trombone was a regular part of the orchestra, but wasn't often put into the spotlight, as Rimsky-Korsakov did with a significant solo for second trombone in *Scheherazade* in 1888.

Gustav Holst gave up playing the piano after suffering neuritis of the hand – and turned to the trombone, sometimes playing in a mock-Viennese brass band.

Trombone players have a few opportunities for solos in the twentieth-century repertoire. Mahler's Third Symphony has a very good solo for trombone, and Ravel's *Boléro* has a particularly hard one. Berg wrote well for the instrument, while his Second Viennese schoolmate Webern wrote unidiomatic passages which are very testing to play. But there are few concertos; apart from Rimsky-Korsakov, whose Concerto is not thought to be one of his best works, the composers who have written for solo trombone and orchestra are not household names: Serocki, Albrechtsberger, Wagenseil and so on. The "trombone concerto" by Leopold Mozart (Wolfgang's father) in about 1759 is not actually a concerto but is movements six to eight of his Serenade in D.

Two of Britain's foremost composers were trombone players: Sir Edward Elgar and Gustav Holst, who took up the instrument after neuritis of the hand prevented him from playing the piano. Elgar's knowledge of the instrument shows in his writing for it which is difficult but not impossible. Further affinity on the part of British composers for the trombone is shown in the Quintet by Sir Malcolm Arnold, and Britten's *War Requiem* and *Young Person's Guide to the Orchestra* which show his clever use of the spacing between the bass trombone and first and second trombones.

The big bands of the 1930s and 1940s typically used to have four trombones, and in terms of playing technique, jazz players have developed the trombone more than their classical counterparts, particularly in the use of mutes and exploiting of timbres. But now it's no surprise to see the same trombonist playing in the symphony hall and in the jazz club; it's all part of the instrument's character.

Perhaps the instrument is so popular with jazz groups not just because of its versatility and expressivity, but also for two more practical reasons: that a) it is loud and b) it is reasonably easy to learn the basics. To make the correct note, just blow a raspberry and slide to one of seven positions that make seven different semitones. To get higher notes, just blow a bit harder; to get slightly higher ones, harder still. Effects like that sliding glissando are very easy to achieve. And because of its simple construction, a new trombone – even a good-quality hand-made one – can cost as little as a reasonable hi-fi system.

While the basic structure of the instrument hasn't changed over the last four hundred years, the quality has certainly improved. Old 'peashooter' trombones, with their small mouthpieces and small bells, cracked up under pressure (anything louder than *mezzo-forte*) to give an unpleasant ripping sound. In the middle of this century American manufacturers increased the bore size of the trombone and enlarged the mouthpieces, leading to an instrument much loved in the 1960s for its big, rich, fat sound. This was ideal for the orchestra in a large hall where the trombone is required to bridge the gap between the tuba and horns, both loud instruments. Jazz trombonists, however, have tended to stay with smaller instruments; they are better suited to the more intimate surround-

A medieval music scene showing the sackbut, an instrument related to the trombone that was then in common use.

ings of the night club or the acoustics of the recording studio, and are less cumbersome to carry around in the back of the drummer's van.

As with most instruments, the national characteristics of a player have become associated with different styles of trombone playing. The French tradition is very soloistic, with a fast vibrato and almost nervy character; the German sound is big, rich and orchestral; the Americans are known for superb technique, bright and brilliant playing; while British playing is more reserved and four-square.

Whatever the style, the technical difficulties are the same. Trombone players must move the slide to an accuracy of perhaps half a centimetre; it can extend out almost a metre from the player and semitones are about eight to 12cm apart. And all this must be done in the time a trumpet player can depress a key. So just to produce the right notes – especially in something like a Brahms chorale – it calls for a lot of precision co-ordination. And a trombonist must be able to read music in a wide variety of forms: the treble clef for brass band work, and the bass, tenor or alto clef for orchestral work.

There isn't much in the solo repertoire for the trombone. However, Christian Lindberg, the world's leading trombone soloist, has commissioned a lot of new works – concertos from Takemitsu, Xenakis and Nyman among others – to add to the repertoire. Another concerto, from his fellow Swede Jan Sandström, written for Lindberg and the conductor Esa-Pekka Salonen, has an interesting story behind the music. The soloist in this *Motorbike Concerto* is, says Lindberg, a "modern Odysseus"; unlike the hero of the Odyssey, however, he does not sail the oceans on a ten-year journey to Ithaca, but drives around the world on a Harley Davidson 883 Sportster, taking in the Everglades in Florida, the mountains in Provence, and Aboriginal Australia on the way. The piece – written for trombone and orchestra but now performed with a digital tape backing – is available on a BIS CD.

An unaccompanied modern masterpiece is *Sequenza V* by Luciano Berio, strongly inspired by a clown called Grock. One day a middle-aged Swiss visited the doctor in a deep depression asking for help. "Go to the theatre", said the physician. "Go and see the clown Grock. He'll cheer you up. He can make anyone laugh." "No good," said the man gloomily, "I am Grock". (The same story is told about another

The No. 1 trombonist **Christian Lindberg** dressed for the part in Sandström's "Motorbike Concerto".

clown, Grimaldi). Berio's work is dedicated to the tragi-comic clown. The only word he used to utter, according to legend, was "why?"; accordingly the piece requires the performer to dress in white and, in the middle of all the quizzical parping and tooting, to stare the audience in the eyes and say, "why?".

Why what? Perhaps the question is why there isn't more of a modern solo repertoire for the trombone. And perhaps the answer is that it doesn't really need it; trombone players wishing to escape from orchestral anonymity can unwind in a jazz solo later on. Angels to nightclub players, orchestral back desks to up-front jazz: the trombone seems happy being played by all sorts of people in all sorts of places.

The Finest Performers

Selected by Simon Hogg, trombonist with the Fine Arts Quintet

Christian Lindberg of Sweden didn't start playing the trombone until the age of 17, after hearing a recording of the jazz trombonist Jack Teagarden, but he's developed into the world's leading player, and is still in his early thirties. He has technical mastery and great expressiveness, and never just plays safe. He manages the impossible by making a living from solo trombone recitals and recordings, and in a way it's a shame that such a good musician doesn't have a greater repertoire to work with.

Two Americans to note are Ron Baron, first trombone of the Boston Symphony Orchestra, and Ralph Sauer, his counterpart in the Los Angeles Symphony Orchestra. Baron is an inspiring player, while Sauer has a meticulous technique. From Eastern Europe, Branimir Slokar is a fine player who has done a lot to promote the instrument, while Vinko Globokar is an important composer-trombonist.

In Britain, John Kenny is an exciting player who has 'done a Lindberg' and gone solo. He makes even avant-garde music come alive and is an excellent player of Berio's *Sequenza*. Ian Bousfield, the first trombone of the London Symphony Orchestra, is another fine player.

On the jazz side, Bill Watrous of America is technically astounding and does quite impossible things with his instrument. He has a huge range and can push a trombone a full octave and a half above and below the official limit. Great names of the past include Tommy Dorsey, a sort of Frank Sinatra of the trombone, who had great control and high range; the very different Jack Teagarden, a loud and exciting player who was a creative improviser; and Roy Williams, a combination of the two styles. In Britain, Don Lusher is well known as a wonderful player who is also a great ambassador for the instrument – a true professional.

The Best CD Recordings

Chosen by Simon Hogg

There isn't much to choose from in the solo trombone catalogue that's available on CD in Britain. Among some excellent recordings by Bill Watrous, is his "Columbia Jazz Odyssey", but that's only available in the US on Columbia. Gerard Schwarz and Ron Baron's recordings are also available only in the US or Europe.

Christian Lindberg is a necessity, and there's a good CD on BIS (CD258) of him playing various works from traditional concertos to avant-garde, including Rimsky's *Flight of the Bumble Bee*! It's an example of the finest trombone playing in the world today. He has several other good recordings on BIS including "The Romantic Trombone" (CD201) "The Winter Trombone" (CD348) "Romantic Trombone Concertos" (CD378) "Solitary Trombone" (CD388) and the *Motorbike Concerto* mentioned in the text.

Branimir Slokar has made a lot of recordings and done a good job selling the instrument to a mass audience. He can be heard on a Claves CD playing works by Wagenseil, Tomasi and Martin (CD50-8407). On another Claves CD he plays baroque concertos and sonatas (CD50-0507).

THE PERCUSSION

The biggest, the loudest, the oldest – and possibly most under-estimated family of orchestral instruments

There are few certainties about the percussion family. No-one can say how many instruments it contains; few of them have agreed playing techniques; and few people could name even one orchestral piece specifically written with percussion in mind. But one thing is certain: percussion is not merely a matter of beating out rhythm.

"There's a great difference between rhythm and feel," says Evelyn Glennie, one of the few percussionists to have made a career as a soloist. "It isn't interesting to see if you can play like a metronome." She has often been frustrated when teaching to have students (and even one conductor) who wanted to be taught to play the drums "to learn rhythm". Too many people, says Glennie, have no concept of different weights or sounds: "you can attack a note, hit it, strike it, tickle it, stroke it, or whatever," she says. "Too many people are not interested in trying to produce any kind of emotion from the instrument," Neil Percy, percussionist with the London Symphony Orchestra, agrees. "If you think the drums are there to hit," he says, "you'll just hit them. You have to think about the sound; playing musically, that's what makes a good percussion player."

Beethoven did much to integrate percussion into the body of the orchestra in his symphonic and other orchestral works.

Percussion is more than a loud sound. As the world's oldest and most widespread family of instruments, it spreads across music from countless different cultures and backgrounds: African drumming, West Indian steel bands, Irish folk, Indian classical, Latin American… the list is endless. A percussionist could probably name you 100 or so instruments given a few minutes and a pencil and paper; the total number played throughout the world – including ethnic instruments played in festivals and ceremonies, and the new percussion devices being developed by makers – may run into tens of thousands. For the artist who, like Glennie, wants to be a "world percussionist", it is clearly an impossible task to be familiar with the whole range. "Percussion is a huge family of instruments," she says, "any of which you might specialise in. Players can dedicate their whole life to timpani; on the other hand I met a chap in Ireland who has been playing the bodhran" – a hand-held drum-like instrument often seen in Irish traditional bands – "for 50 years! Percussion is a never-ending journey," she says. "By the time I'm 90 there's still no way I'll know everything. I am always going to be a kid, always to be learning."

And learning an instrument doesn't just involve technique. "It's crucial to know all about the instrument," she says: "how it's made, what it's made of, and the sort of music played with it – there has to be that understanding first." Unlike Western classical music, many ethnic-derived types of music have no strictly defined technique. "A lot of percussion playing has to do with imagination," she says. "There isn't above a certain level any more a right or a wrong way – it's up to you to use the instrument."

Which is not to say that a percussion player can please themselves as to how they play. "Percussion is the backbone of the music," says Glennie. "If that's gone, the whole thing collapses." And that's true whether the music happens to be ethnic, jazz, rock, classical or whatever. With her experience of 'world music', Glennie can relate techniques across boundaries: Japanese traditional to Western classical, for example, or Irish folk to Latin American. "Each thing influences the other: you can relate bodhran playing to conga playing, for example. Bodhran playing is so incredibly relaxed – it's like shaking your hand out, like a timpani roll. You let your hand fall on bodhran, as you let your hands fall on timpani."

The choice of soft to hard heads for the sticks used on drums can significantly change the sound produced, and forms an endless source of debate for performers.

The two most astonishing examples of percussion techniques Glennie believes are shown in two very different types of music: Indian classical, where a tabla player can produce unbelievably complex rhythmic patterns, and Scots drumming, another area that players can spend a lifetime perfecting. As a Scot herself, she may of course be well disposed to Caledonian music! Glennie points out the link between the rhythms of speech and the feel of a

culture's music. "You only have to listen to an Indian speaking, and then watch a tabla player, to see the rhythms wriggling through them. It's in their whole approach." It's in British music too, she says: listen to the way "Dunbar" is pronounced by an English speaker ("*Dun*-bar") and a Scots speaker ("Dun-*bar*") and then listen to rhythms of each country's folk music. Scots drumming often relies on the 'da-daa' figure, called the 'Scotch snap'; an English folk-based tune such as "Land of Hope and Glory" has the opposite pattern of stress.

The influence of 'world percussion' is slowly having an effect on the music colleges. In the past a percussion student would study the orchestral mainstays – timpani (often called kettledrums), bass and side drums, cymbals, triangle, tambourine and so on – and the tuned percussion instruments such as xylophone, marimba and glockenspiel. (The celesta, though classed as a percussion instrument, has a keyboard and is usually played in orchestras by a pianist).

Now, however, colleges are bringing in specialists from outside to teach additional areas of percussion – a Latin American expert to teach congas and bongos, for example. Glennie cites the Royal Northern College of Music as particularly good in its willingness to embrace many different styles of percussion in the syllabus.

Neil Percy is keen to stress how useful this diversity is. "It gives you an understanding of the whole spectrum," he says. It's also vital for a percussionist to be versatile: players like Percy can find themselves playing timpani in a Beethoven symphony one evening, kit drums in a Gershwin pop evening with rock singer Randy Crawford the next, and congas in an advertising jingle session the following afternoon. Unlike percussionists in American orchestras who tend to specialise, those in British orchestras must be more general. "You never know what instrument you're going to play tomorrow," says Percy, adding that the differences are not just of technique. "Unlike timpani, kit drums set the pace for everyone else. Conductors must be aware of the fact that a good orchestra will therefore be listening to the drums and not just following the baton."

Despite this broadening out of percussion playing, orchestral playing – mainly timpani – remains the basis for most music a percussionist will encounter. It's quite possible to specialise in timpani playing, and the development of the orchestral drum sub-family could take up a book in itself.

The origins of orchestral drums lie in three main sources. The Crusades of 1100 to 1300 brought the kettledrum to Europe; the craze for 'Turkish music' in the eighteenth century introduced a variety of more noisy military drums; and the first part of this century saw Afro-American influences bringing more exotic instruments.

The eastern origin of kettledrums shows in their old name. What Shakespeare (in *Hamlet*) calls kettledrums, Chaucer (in *The Canterbury Tales*) calls "nakeres", deriving from the Turkish naqqareh. The original nakers (as the spelling became) were two small drums held between the players legs. The obvious resemblance to a part of the male anatomy ensured that the word – pronounced to rhyme with "crackers" – became a slang term for it.

Kettledrums did little in early music. In 1692 Purcell was one of the first composers to specify the instrument as part of an orchestra in his *Fairy Queen*; there was even a brief solo for the kettledrum. A Bach cantata *Tönet, ihr Pauken! Erschallet Trompetten!* also demands a short solo, and Handel used 16 kettledrums and 12 side drums in the performance of his *Firework Music* in 1749 – the extra volume being necessary for this outdoor performance, and perhaps to be heard above the crackle of the wooden pavilion which burnt down after a firework had set it alight!

A glimpse of the universality of percussion: Peking; native Americans; a cowboy type, who doesn't really count as a native culture; Thailand; Ghana; Senegal and South Korea

Evelyn Glennie has put solo percussion on the popular map with many TV and radio appearances and several recordings.

Mozart had written a divertimento of about 1773 that called for four kettle-drums tuned to four different notes, but this was a rare foray into melody for the instrument; basically the drum was used to provide a military feel and not to supply any musical material, as in Haydn's famous *Drum-roll* Symphony.

It was Beethoven who, musically speaking, really integrated the timpani into the rest of orchestra. The early years of the nineteenth century saw the percussion used more and more in the orchestra, usually providing very simple bass notes (just tonic and dominant). But Beethoven's use of the timpani to provide a musical bass line changed the instrument, and the sound of orchestra as a whole. By playing thematic material instead of rhythmic banging, the orchestral palette had been dramatically broadened. He used revolutionary tunings for the drums in many of his works. (The opera *Fidelio* calls for a diminished fifth, A-E flat; the Seventh Symphony for a minor sixth, A-F; the Eighth Symphony for octave Fs). He developed writing through his nine symphonies, and the second movement of the Ninth Symphony shows how the timpani had become instrumental instead of just rhythmic. The work is therefore popular with timpanists, who have challenging lines which contribute to the musical framework, instead of bare rhythms.

The next big steps were made by Hector Berlioz in the mid 1800s. He stretched the musical possibilities of the timpani further by having more and more players each with differently tuned instruments: the *Symphonie fantastique* of 1830 required four kettledrums and four players, and the "March to the Scaffold" is a showpiece of percussion playing; while his Requiem of 1837 originally demanded 16 players with 32 kettledrums – a figure subsequently halved through sheer practicality.

Modern works can demand very intricate tunings. Fortunately modern instruments are more reliable than they were in Beethoven's time, when the "heads" – the part of the timpani that is stretched over the bowl – were made of calf-skin. This is so reactive to moisture that a slight change in the weather can throw the tuning and tone completely out, as percussionists using authentic instruments in modern concerts know only too well when the air-conditioning in the Barbican blows in moisture-laden water from the Thames. Plastic replaced calf-skin in the 1960s and is unaffected by the atmosphere. It also has the advantage of being louder and less breakable in energetic pieces; calf-skin heads are often preferred for recording, however, because of their warmer and dryer sound which can work better in the studio.

Timpani playing is the bread-and-butter of the percussionist. There are of course countless other instruments, but few of them can claim to be as genuinely part of the orchestra. Many of the more exotic instruments are used for one-off special effects, or even as gimmicks: Bizet used castanets in his opera *Carmen* to set the Spanish atmosphere; Wagner used a collection of anvils in his opera *Das Rheingold* to suggest the labyrinthine burrowing of the enslaved Nibelungen; Schoenberg asked for "some big iron chains" in his massive *Gurrelieder* of 1911; Satie even used an office typewriter in his ballet *Parade*. Modern works can demand such exotic effects as "scratch strings [of piano] lengthwise along winding, with a coin held like a banjo pick" (William Russell's *Fugue for Eight Percussion Instruments* of 1933).

Percussion has become, in various guises, an indispensable part of the modern orchestra. But for the solo percussionist there is little in the way of worthwhile solo repertoire. There are a few concertos for one of the most expressive of tuned percussion instruments, the marimba; this is similar to a xylophone in having wooden bars that are struck by mallets, but gets its deeper and softer tone from the softer mallets used and a metal resonating chamber. There are concertos by Akira Miyoshi, Richard Rodney Bennett, Paul Creston, Andrzej Panufnik and André Jolivet for marimba (or vibraphone or other percussion) but few are as well-known as they should be. There is virtually nothing by a "big name" composer (apart from Milhaud's two concertos, one for vibraphone and one for percussion, neither of which are great pieces); Varèse's *Ionisation* and Stockhausen's *Zyklus* are major modern works for percussion, but are not easy listening. And what repertoire there is can be difficult to obtain in Britain, even though the sheet music is easily found abroad.

Further problems for the solo percussionist are the practicalities of affording, storing and maintaining the dozens of different instruments needed. A marimba alone can cost as much as a small car, and the organisational headaches of moving a xylophone, marimba, vibraphone, timpani, various bass and side drums and dozens of other pieces by van on a concert tour are obvious. Practising isn't easy either; Glennie's long-suffering neighbours in her London flat have had to learn to live with the constant vibrations from her basement.

Yet, with the influences of world music and ever-broadening interest in the percussion family, there are more percussion students than ever, with an increasingly wide choice of areas to specialise in. Percussionists tend to be confident people; there's no other option when a duff note or wrong entry on your instrument will be noticed rather more than it would be in the second violins. The future of percussion looks confident too.

THE FINEST PERFORMERS

Selected by Neil Percy, percussionist with the London Symphony Orchestra

Jimmy Holland with the BBC Symphony Orchestra has been around for longer than anyone else. He's one of the longest serving and most experienced percussionists in the world. He was with the BBC SO during the "golden period" when Messiaen and Boulez were working with them.

A marvellous character and very important figure, especially in teaching, is James Blades who has taught at the Royal Academy of Music. He's been a great influence on everyone.

The standard of percussion playing is high in Britain and I've always been impressed with provincial standards. Alan Cumberland's approach has always been musical; his awareness of what fits and what doesn't and his desire to make music always impresses me. Dave Hassel of Manchester has made a great contribution to teaching and made great efforts as a player with again a very musical approach. He's a Latin American specialist, and you'll have heard him dozens of times on commercial music.

Finally Evelyn Glennie has given a focal point to solo percussion playing and made a lot of people think. What she does she does very well.

THE BEST CD RECORDINGS

Chosen by Neil Percy

The set of Beethoven symphonies shows the development of percussion writing – if you listen to them in sequence you'll be amazed by what the percussion is doing at the end. Beethoven's Ninth Symphony went furthest in breaking new ground for the timpani because it integrates them into the melodic material instead of just providing a beat. I like the Karajan set with the Berlin Philharmonic Orchestra (Deutsche Grammophon 415 832-2).

Rimsky-Korsakov's *Scheherazade* makes great technical demands on the snare drum. So much so, in fact, that it's often used as an audition piece – which leads one or two snare drum players to play too loud in concert! What the percussion section is asked to do as a unit uses very complex patterns, very different from the writing up till then. When it works it really works, especially the last movement. Bernstein's version with the New York Philharmonic is interesting (Sony CD47605, coupled with Stravinsky's *Firebird*).

Many of Mahler's symphonies use percussion to good effect, and the Second Symphony uses it not only to provide rhythmic reinforcement but also to provide thematic material. It doesn't have a lot to do, but it's good writing. When the percussion comes in you know

about it! It's good to play too, and can be very rewarding (Gilbert Kaplan on Pickwick DPCD910).

To many people, "percussion" means "timpani" – and "timpani" means "kettledrums".

To show what the percussion section is capable of, Stravinsky's *Rite of Spring* ballet music is a fabulous piece of writing, expressive and forceful. The bass drum and timpani are at the heart of it, providing a strong pivot to the dance (DG 415 854-2).

Bartók's *Music for Strings, Percussion and Celesta* is a modern showcase that pushes the percussion to the fore, as he does in the *Concerto for Orchestra* (Decca 421 443-2).

THE HARPSICHORD

More than just a poor relation of the piano

The sound of the harpsichord is something you either love or hate. One critic thought it "a performance on a bird-cage with a toasting-fork"; it reminded Sir Thomas Beecham of "two skeletons copulating on a tin roof".

The trouble with the harpsichord, since its appearance in the 1500s, has always been the lack of dynamic range, an inescapable product of the plucked-string mechanics of the instrument. When a key is pressed, a tiny plectrum embedded in a wooden 'jack' rises past the metal string. It plucks it on the way up and then falls back down, with an escapement mechanism moving it out the way so as not to pluck the string again. This means that any key press, from a caress to a clobber, comes out at just about the same volume. Effects of crescendo and diminuendo are therefore only possible by increasing or decreasing the number of notes being played at one time, presenting serious limitations for the composer and player.

It was this lack of expressive power that caused the demise of the harpsichord. In the first half of the eighteenth century a new keyboard instrument appeared, in which the strings were struck, not plucked. This gave the performer complete control over the loudness of each note: a caress could sound like caress, a clobber like a clobber. The very name of the new instrument was chosen for sound marketing reasons, to emphasise its superiority: pianoforte, 'soft and loud'. Various people helped with the development, from Cristofori in 1709 with his struck-string harpsichord, to Silbermann in 1726, who built two pianos for J S Bach. Whoever is credited, the new expressiveness available to composers and performers changed the face of music: the volcanic force of a late Beethoven sonata, for example, simply wouldn't come across on a harpsichord.

But this is to ignore the astonishing wealth of music written for the harpsichord which, before being pushed into obscurity by the piano, was the most familiar and important domestic instrument.

This had been the case ever since the late 1500s, when the harpsi-

J S Bach had two pianos made for him – but whether his keyboard music works better on harpsichord or piano is a matter of taste.

chord had established itself as the major domestic keyboard. It was seen as very much a genteel instrument, ideal for young ladies to learn, as well as being practical: its big rival, the clavichord, had too small a sound to use in even medium sized rooms, while the chamber organ was not really portable enough to be convenient. So the harpsichord, along with its smaller relatives the virginal and the spinet, became the most familiar instrument in the home, and hence the one with which most people began their musical education. Mainly because of this, there was a great amount of excellent music written for the harpsichord, catering for everyone from beginners to experts. The Mulliner Book was a significant early collection of pieces, some of them very athletic, and the Fitzwilliam Virginal Book contained some extraordinarily virtuosic solos by composers such as William Byrd, Orlando Gibbons and John Bull.

More striking music was written in the 1600s. Frescobaldi's works present many technical and harmonic demands, and his music is perhaps not as well known as it ought to be. Towards the end of the century Henry Purcell wrote many charming pieces which are a good introduction to the sound of the seventeenth-century instrument.

The harpsichord carved out a place for itself in the seventeenth and eighteenth-century orchestra as a continuo instrument – supplying a constant rhythmic background for the rest of the ensemble. Without the bite of the plucked string sound, it is surprising how music for a small orchestra can seem to lack drive. But the most solid additions to the solo repertoire came from three major composers all born in the same year, 1685: J S Bach and Handel of north Germany, and Domenico Scarlatti of Italy.

Bach's huge output included several major harpsichord works: the Partitas, the French and English suites, and the *Italian Concerto*. He also wrote the *Goldberg Variations* for one of his star pupils, Johann Goldberg. The music was for a count who suffered from insomnia and wanted this substantial work played to him during his sleepless nights. Far from

Domenico Scarlatti wrote 555 sonatas for the harpsichord, some of them way ahead of their time.

being sleep-inducing, the work is one of the richest ever written for the harpsichord and a standard work of the repertoire.

But perhaps Bach's most famous harpsichord collection is the mighty set of *48 Preludes and Fugues*. Each book of 24 consists of a prelude and fugue in each of the 12 major and 12 minor keys. The exact purpose of the work is still open to interpretation by scholars. At the time there were various ways of tuning the harpsichord (or any keyboard instrument). Most would make a few keys sound very smooth and others sound rough and slightly out of tune, but the "equal temperament" system was a sort of compromise where all keys sounded equally smooth (or, for those with unusually musical ears, equally rough). Bach called his showpiece *Das wohltemperierte Klavier*, or "The Well-Tempered Clavier". With its exhaustive coverage of keys it was clearly designed to show off the merits of the tuning system – but which one, the system that made all keys equal, or the one which gave different keys their own character?

The equal temperament system was the one adopted as standard for all keyboards. Virtually all the recordings of the *48* you will hear, whether on harpsichord or piano, are on that system, but whatever Bach intended, the set is a comprehensive collection of compositional styles of the day. One of the pieces – the first Prelude in C major – has become familiar as the piano accompaniment in the song *Ave Maria*, written by Gounod in 1859.

Handel's eight great Suites for the harpsichord show more variety than Bach, but for sheer virtuosity and originality, the Scarlatti Sonatas stand out most of all. They form probably the biggest collection of pieces for any instrument ever written: Ralph Kirkpatrick catalogued 555 of them. Scarlatti called the earlier ones *essercizi*, or 'exercises', and wrote most of them in Spain during the last years of his life, between 1729 and 1757. They use a staggering variety of effects that seem surprisingly modern. Some are technical, such as crossing the hands while playing; some are harmonic, and show the influence of the Spanish guitar with resonating 'open strings' appearing in the music (indeed many of his pieces can be played well on the guitar with little adjustment). The Sonata, K175, in particular is bizarre, and contains crunchy-sounding clusters of notes that look on paper as though they couldn't possibly have been written before the twentieth century.

In France, Rameau and the Couperin family were writing a lot of pieces for the instrument that are a basic part of the concert repertoire today. But the days of the harpsichord were numbered. François Couperin, perhaps the most accomplished of the family, had written in 1713 on the problems caused by the lack of volume control on the instrument, saying the solution lay in the player's "infinite art supported by fine taste". Instead, the pianoforte arrived a few years later. Many compositions written in the late 1700s by composers such as Haydn, Mozart and C P E Bach (the most searching of J S Bach's composer sons) are rather ambiguous in that it isn't clear whether they were written for the piano or the harpsichord. When Beethoven's *Moonlight* Sonata was written in 1801, it was intended for either piano, clavichord or harpsichord – not because it sounds particularly good on the harpsichord, but because the instrument was still likely to be found in a front room at the time, and a publisher had to address the market.

But the piano was rapidly gaining favour, and the harpsichord makers desperately tried to compete by adding more and more technical modifications to the basic machinery. A number of effects had long been employed to give variety such as switching in different sets of strings to give different sounds. As well as having alternative sets of strings that could be switched in called eight- and four-foot stops (the nomenclature was taken from the organ: there were no strings of that length anywhere on the frame) models were now being built with up to half a dozen extra effects. Some makers added 'lute stops' where the plectra were situated at the very edge of the string to give a dry, nasal, lute-like sound; others tried 'harp stops', where small pieces of leather slightly dampened the strings to give a soft, harp-like effect. Some even tried to bolt on a volume control in a Venetian blind arrangement that could be opened or closed to vary the amount of sound coming out – with limited success. All these could be switched in by organ-like stops or pedals, and many harpsichords offered two manuals so that two effects could be used at once or in immediate succession, even though 98 per cent of all pieces ever written can be played on a one-manual instrument.

But it was a losing battle, and the ability of the piano to shape a phrase couldn't be matched by any amount of Heath Robinson engineering. Shortly after the turn of the century the harpsichord had been swept aside, and until the 1900s it was a forgotten instrument, totally ignored by players and romantic composers alike.

But the twentieth century saw a revival on the new Pleyel harpsichord, an iron-framed and pedalled instrument structurally similar to a piano, made famous by pianist turned harpsichordist Wanda Landowska. Manual de Falla wrote the first modern Harpsichord Concerto, and Francis Poulenc followed with his *Concert champêtre* that gently pokes fun at eighteenth-century harpsichord styles. Other works were written by Frank Martin and Walter Leigh, an English composer killed in action in Libya in 1942, whose gem of a *Concertino* has been unaccountably ignored. Another underrated modern work is the Satie-esque set of pieces called *Insectarium* by Jean Françaix. Not all the attempts to build a modern repertoire were successful though. Frederick Delius wrote for the instrument, but was obviously under the impression that the harpsichord has a sustaining pedal, like the piano, making his piece effectively unplayable!

In the last two decades there has been something of a revival in the fortunes of the harpsichord, not only through recordings, but also in the music col-

The decoration on a **harpsichord** is traditionally a very important part of the instrument.

leges and academies. Much of this is due to the resurgence of interest in early music – almost all the harpsichords made now are copies of early instruments. (In fact, if you wanted to play Falla's Concerto on the instrument he wrote it for, you'd be in trouble – there are only a handful of Pleyels left. Modern harpsichords are in much shorter supply than 'period' instruments).

"The harpsichord is now doing very well indeed," says Virginia Black, who teaches at the Royal Academy of Music in London. "In the last few years it's built up enormously."

The prospects for harpsichord players are getting better too. "I feel quite happy about encouraging my students whether they're going into continuo, solo or duo playing," she says. She is a successful performer herself, in duos with her husband Howard Davies, who plays baroque violin, and in solo recitals.

Her exciting style has no doubt helped the recent surge of interest in this sort of programme, and she enjoys the reaction of audiences who come with preconceptions of the harpsichord. "Some people have the feeling that it's rather dull. Partly this is a residue of the early harpsichord playing of the 1950s and 1960s when programmes tended to be dry and dusty, and partly because the most familiar place to see the harpsichord is in continuo playing, when it doesn't stand out. But after a concert, people come up and say they can't believe how exciting the music is."

The usual way into the harpsichord is from the piano. Many players go to one of the music colleges to study the piano and take the harpsichord as a supporting subject. Then many find that, in studying the instrument that much of the music already familiar to them was intended for, like Virginia Black they "get hooked". But the pianist coming to the harpsichord has to radically re-think their technique: no sustaining pedals and no control over the 'touch' of the keyboard.

"You can't underestimate the challenge of making an instrument that seems so intractable do the things a piano can do," says Black. Without any control of the volume, the harpsichord player has to use a variety of methods to give expression, and the illusion of line, of crescendo and diminuendo: shaping a phrase by the timing of the notes rather than the 'touch', or subtly swelling the sound by holding some notes of a chord slightly longer than might be expected. (Some harpsichord composers, such as Couperin, wrote these effects very precisely into their music).

She likes to show two very different facets of the instrument. "Playing expressively is an exciting challenge, but equally I like to show it off in its more exciting and virtuosic form – Soler, Scarlatti, and the major Bach works. The Toccata in D or *Chromatic Fantasia and Fugue* are very different from each other, but they're massive in impact."

Black recorded the complete works of Rameau on Collins Classics. She uses a modern copy of a 1740s model harpsichord, made by one of the leading modern makers, Andrew Garlick. "I'd say he's the best in the country," says Black. "He has a real feeling for sound, which is the most important thing for the performer, but he also makes them look very beautiful."

There are a lot of mechanics in a harpsichord and it's not always easy to find quality materials: the best plectra are made from quills, with those from the raven (now virtually extinct in Britain) and the South American condor being preferred.

Much as with wines, connoisseurs of the harpsichord can identify a period instrument's nationality by its sound. (Some even assert that Bach cannot be played to sound right on a French model, nor Rameau on an English instrument, for example.) Italian harpsichords have a crisp, dry sound; models of the French school, deriving from the famous Flemish family of makers, Ruckers, are said to sound glowing and opulent. English harpsichords have been criticised by some as being "too good" – eighteenth-century models made by Schudi and Kirkman give such a rich and long-lasting sound that they give the effect of the modern instrument's 16-foot stop.

The revival of interest in early music has helped re-establish the instrument. But Stephen Dodgson, one of the few composers who writes modern music for the harpsichord, believes that many players look to the past too much.

"The problem is that players never think of anything except seventeenth- and eighteenth-century music," he says. Dodgson has swelled the modern repertoire himself with concertos, various chamber music works and sets of solo inventions.

He believes that the harpsichord has a lot to offer the modern composer, contrary to its image as an inferior and colourless relative of the piano. "I write for the piano too but never regard them as interchangeable," he says. "The harpsichord has a different spacing. Because of the difference in string size between treble and bass, the harpsichord has an extraordinary colouristic and textural range, bigger than people believe". He was influenced by Scarlatti's music when he started writing for the instrument and points out that no-one complains about lack of colour there.

"What we need is players who will view the contemporary possibilities more actively, and not bury

Virginia Black is one of the leading modern players of the harpsichord, whose recordings are highly regarded by the music critics.

themselves in the past. It would do them good, and extend their range. Composers have also got to do something. They must look at the instrument for what it is, and draw the music out. If they do that, then both sides can benefit."

The Finest Performers

Selected by Kenneth Mobbs, a harpsichord specialist and historian

Wanda Landowska was a Polish pianist, and her harpsichord playing is a good example of the big early-twentieth-century instrument, rather than modern copies. She made the music incredibly interesting, playing with great fire, and is remarkable for her sheer dedication to the music. Unfortunately there's only one example of her playing on CD at the moment, a recording of *The Well-Tempered Clavier*.

Another excellent player of the modern English harpsichord is George Malcolm, an absolute wizard who uses all the pedals and "special effects" of the modern instrument – eight and four-foot stops, couplers, everything. He was the main performer of the 1950s and 1960s but seems to have been overlooked in the CD catalogue.

For sheer authenticity and scholarship I would pick the Dutchman Gustav Leonhardt and Kenneth Gilbert from Canada. Gilbert has tremendous historical knowledge and is a very intelligent all-rounder, but he's particularly strong on the French style, and has edited editions of Couperin and Rameau.

Scott Ross of America was an unforgettable player. He recorded all 555 Scarlatti sonatas in one year, an incredible achievement, and used to play them in concert from memory.

Of the younger generation I like Virginia Black. She teaches harpsichord at the Royal Academy as well as performing and recording regularly, and produces some very exciting stuff.

Finally, a name to watch out for is Nicholas Parle, an interesting young Australian player who won a recent international competition at Bruges and has enormous natural gifts.

The Best CD Recordings

Chosen by Kenneth Mobbs

If you want a particular suite of Couperin's, the *Eighth Order* is the one to start with. It's the consummation of the standard French suite with a magnificent passacaglia at the end. After this point the pieces become more fanciful descriptive pieces. Kenneth Gilbert has recorded *Orders* six to 12, the whole of Couperin's second book of pieces, on Harmonia Mundi (HMA 190 354/6, three CDs).

Rameau's 1728 Suite in A minor is a big set of variations which get very athletic. It's a striking piece, and I've always been impressed with the performance of Trevor Pinnock, who has recorded it on CRD with the 1724 Suite in E minor (CRD 3310).

One of the most famous harpsichord pieces is Handel's *Harmonious Blacksmith* Variations, which is part of the fifth of his eight suites for harpsichord. Try Trevor Pinnock's CRD recording: CRD 3307.

There are many recordings of the Scarlatti sonatas and Colin Tilney's Dorian CD has a wide range from No. 2 to No. 418, including the odd No. 175. He's a very authoritative player and I've always been impressed by him (Dorian DOR 90103).

There are few recordings of twentieth-century harpsichord pieces. It's a pity that the Falla Concerto or the two Martin pieces with orchestra are not on CD. However, the Poulenc *Concert champêtre* is available on Erato, played by Ton Koopman. It's coupled with the Poulenc Organ Concerto, which is a great piece (2292-45233-2).

THE HARP

A classical renaissance

The **harp** is one of the oldest instruments, as the pre-Raphaelites well knew: this picture of an Egyptian court shows the instrument.

The harp is one of the oldest instruments. Pictures from the pyramids show that there were harpists in Ancient Egypt, which had some of the first recorded professional musicians over four-and-a-half thousand years ago.

"It's the most fantastic instrument," says recitalist David Watkins, who teaches harp at the Guildhall School of Music in London. "It has all the possibilities and colours of a keyboard instrument, but has the sheer physical pleasure of bare hands on strings; intellectually, technically and sensually, it's wonderful to play. It's also beautiful to look at." Clive Morley, whose family has made some of the world's best harps for over a hundred years, puts it more simply. "It's perfection," he says.

Many would agree: the ethereal sound has made the harp the traditional instrument played in artists' impressions of heaven since its appearance in prehistoric times. But in the 1950s heaven was about the only place left where it was being played: the harp had fallen so far out of favour, Morley recalls, that the UK market required one new instrument per year, and the total number of earthbound professional players could just about be assembled on the point of the pin. Fortunately for this distinguished instrument, it's now on the way back up, re-established as a concert and recording instrument.

The origin of the harp is as shimmering and elusive as the sound of its echoing strings; just about every culture has had some sort of musical device based on a few strings stretched over a soundbox, but trying to trace back a distinct lineage leading to the modern harp is virtually impossible. Magically – as if accompanied by a swirling glissando – we cut to the early 1600s, where up pops the harp.

Or rather, up pop several different folk harps. There was no standardisation even within one country, with the designs and specifications of an instrument being up to the maker. The clarsach or Scottish harp, for example, was a small instrument with strings of wire, gut or horsehair – anything that was available – and irregular spacing between the strings at the whim of the maker. The Irish harp was similar but larger. These instruments were restricted to the notes of a scale, with no accidentals – as if a pianist were allowed to play only the white notes on the keyboard. This suited folk music pretty well (perhaps even shaped it to some extent) in being "modal" – that is, made up solely of "white notes", with the only variation being on which note your scale would start or end. It's usually the modal nature of the scale used that gives a folk tune its characteristically bouncy folk sound.

However, it is natural for composers to want to explore new musical territory, and some harps were made with extra strings to supply the missing notes. The Italian harp had two sets of strings, while the Welsh harp (the telyn) had three: two identical outer sets of naturals with the sharps (equivalent to the black notes on a piano) tucked between them, meaning the player had to stick a finger in between two outer strings to pluck one of the inner set. The doubling of the natural notes meant it was possible to achieve effects of the same note repeating by rapidly alternating the note played on one set with the same note played on the other. As makers developed their skills they started to introduce

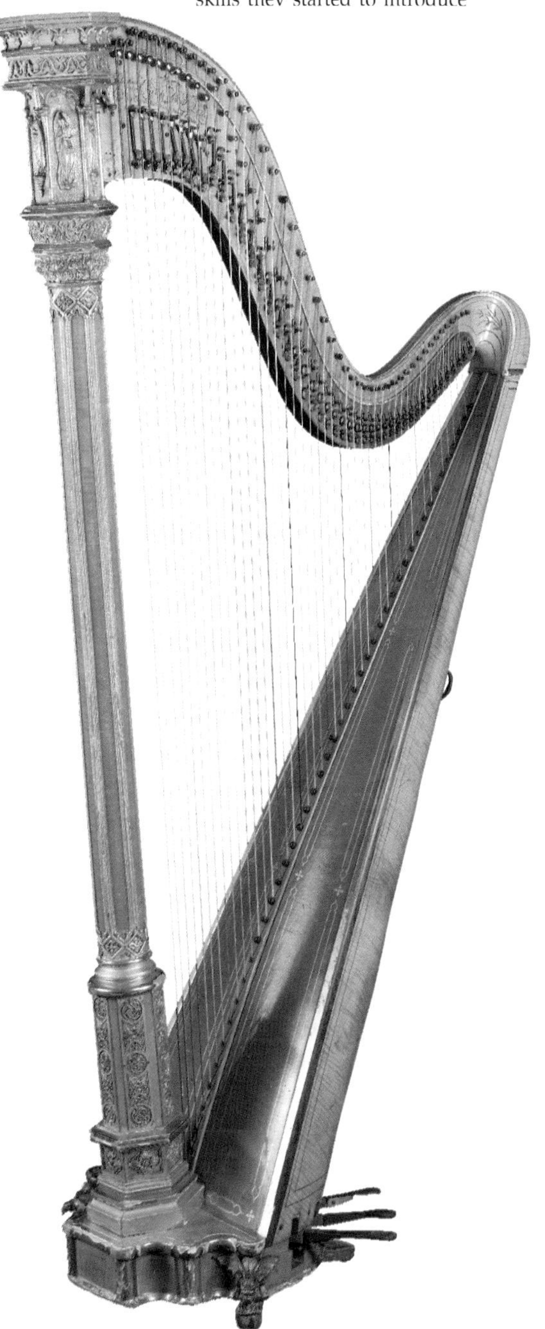

tiny hooks or blades above each string which the player could turn round to sharpen that string by a semitone. Modern folk harps still use this system.

At this stage the harp was very much a folk instrument, played by a local or travelling bard who might have served as a source of news as well as a musician. (Such travelling harpists, particularly in Ireland, were bound to be at the focal point of rebellions – so much so that the harp went through periods of being banned!) Music was mainly passed down by ear, though some early compositions survive in tablature (giving the performer a diagrammatic list of the strings to pluck, rather than notes on a stave). One significant early collection in tablature, the ap Huw manuscript, is still not fully understood. In the 1700s some harp players rescued old folk tunes and wrote them down in conventional music notation. Bunting's *History of the Harp* collected Irish compositions; Edward Jones produced a volume of Welsh tunes in 1784. Over a hundred years later Sir Edward Armstrong was to gather and re-arrange music included in these early collections, and many of the "traditional Irish folk tunes" we hear today have come from this source. Turlough Carolan (1670–1738), the blind Irish folk harpist, wrote over 200 tunes – many of them still turning up on TV or in adverts in various arrangements – though his name is probably best known nowadays for the cream and whisky liqueur named after him.

In the early 1800s, the upwardly mobile harp was leaving its roots fast and becoming the favourite instrument of the ruling classes. Skills in metalwork gathered from gun and rifle making were being used in harp manufacture, and new mechanisms were developed whereby a harpist could depress a single pedal to sharpen a whole set of notes at once: by moving all the Fs up a step the harp would move from the key of C to the key of G, for example. The ability to change key wholesale, instead of just changing one note – and hence now be able to modulate easily and give shape and development to a composition – opened up harp music. Harps with seven pedals – one flattening or sharpening a particular set of notes – could play in any key, and compete with any keyboard instrument in their ability to play the new romantic style of music that ranged chromatically over many different keys. Modern concert harps are still based on this pattern.

If you had been a guest at any country house or mansion in the early 1800s, you'd have been treated to some sort of musical performance (and probably invited to take part too). Oliver Davis of the Royal College of Music has a special interest in this "stately home music" of the 1800s. "Music was ringing through these houses all the time," he says, "and it's evident in the sensationally difficult harp music written even for amateurs, such as the Duke of Wellington's relatives, that they were very accomplished players, even though the harp of the period had slacker strings and was easier to play fast than those of today."

With its elegant shape and gentle sound, the harp was just the right sort of instrument for a genteel young lady to play, and the ledgers of makers Erard show the majority of the 6,000 harps they made that century were being delivered to Lady Carolines and Baroness Elizabeths. The harp was booming – particularly the new louder instruments being designed for use in large salons and concert-halls where they would have to be heard in larger and larger ensembles.

The repertoire was pretty small, though. The harp had been used in Italian opera as early as the 1600s, but the musical limitations and folky image meant that major composers continued either to ignore the harp or include it grudgingly in orchestral works for a few swirly "special effects" – this despite the fact that Haydn, Weber, Rossini, Liszt, Chopin

and Mendelssohn are all known to have been harp players.

Turlogh Carolan the Irish harp performer and composer whose name is celebrated in a liqueur.

Bach, for example, never wrote for the harp at all; Handel used it a few times, but reportedly as much to provide work for two Welshmen called Powell than anything else; Haydn never used it orchestrally but wrote a sonata for flute, harp and double-bass; Mozart wrote just one harp work, a Concerto for flute and harp; Beethoven's singular contribution to the harp repertoire was to provide a harp part in his music to *Prometheus*.

Some romantic composers were keener on the harp. Mendelssohn, Schumann and Brahms rarely used it, but Berlioz, Liszt and Wagner often did;

Marisa Robles of Spain is probably the most famous modern player of the harp thanks to her many recordings of the standard repertoire.

for example, the finale in Wagner's *Das Rheingold* utilises six harpists all playing independent arpeggios so that the gods may enter Valhalla to the sound of heavenly music.

But the salon player of the 1800s generally had to rely on music of varying quality written by some of the well-known composer harpists of the time (or, as some say rather pointedly, harpist composers). One of the most colourful of these was Nicolas Bochsa (1787–1856), who is often said to have perfected modern harp technique. He started as the official harpist to Louis XVIII and Napoleon, but was sentenced in 1817 to 12 years' jail on being found guilty of forgery to the tune of £30,000 (taking the cost of a new concert harp as a yardstick, this would be equivalent to around £6 million today). Fortunately he was out of the country at the time (and extradition was still many decades away) so he went to London instead of returning. There he got a teaching post at the Royal Academy of Music in 1822, committed bigamy, ran off with another composer's wife, toured the Old and New World as a virtuoso performer, and as a finale wrote the Requiem performed at his own funeral in Australia.

A harpist with a less interesting life, but who wrote more interesting music, was Elias Parrish Alvars of Teignmouth, Devon (1808–1849) – the English "Liszt of the harp" as Berlioz called him. A much-admired friend of Liszt, Berlioz and Chopin, he wrote hundreds of harp pieces, many of which were lost in his lifetime and have only recently been discovered. His style, influenced by Bochsa, took harp playing to heights of virtuosity hitherto unattained (and possibly unsurpassed since). Inspired by the romantic movement in music, he made full use of the ability of the double-action harp to change keys and hence modulate, giving his compositions a depth never seen in folk-inspired harp tunes.

David Watkins is one of the many harp recitalists who include his works in his performances, and has recorded a set of recently rediscovered Romances by Parish Alvars for Virgin. The manuscripts are now in the care of Clive Morley's harp library in Gloucestershire, and going through these hidden masterpieces has provided Watkins with hours of delight. "We found so much fabulous stuff. There's some wonderful music lurking there," says Watkins, "and a tremendous addition to the repertoire."

The prospect of an hour or more of harp music, whether on CD or in a recital, sounds dangerously like six courses of prawn cocktail, but Watkins believes there is plenty of variation within Parish Alvars's music to sustain interest. "It's like listening to an hour of piano music, or any solo instrument," he says. "You need a variety of resonances. It can be difficult on the harp, but it's quite possible." Certainly the range of resonances within the pieces Watkins selected for the recording shows plenty of variety: hints of Liszt at times, Gluck at others, covering the range of harp possibilities from the blatantly showy to the subtly poetic.

Another set of undiscovered works in Morley's library was written by Philippe Meyer, a contemporary of Mozart. Four harp sonatas were found which Watkins describes as "as good as Mozart or Haydn".

In the twentieth century, the harp quickly lost favour. The mass-produced piano, cheaper than a harp and with a far more substantial repertoire, had become the instrument of the salon and front room. A couple of solid additions to the chamber repertoire had come from Debussy and Ravel, but new harp music was as rare as the number of professional players. The nadir was probably in the 1940s, when Sir George Dyson of the Royal College of Music decided it was time for a clear-out of the College's collection of instruments that students could borrow. Two dozen harps – perhaps a quarter of a million pounds' worth at today's insurance value – weren't being used, so they were simply chopped up and binned.

Since the 1970s, though, the harp has suddenly come back. The renaissance has been startling: demand for the instrument has been fuelled not only by a combination of recordings, radio and TV, but also by wedding receptions, restaurants and hotel salons. The use of the harp to provide pretty background sounds that echo around the lobbies of Hiltons and Ritzes around the world may not have drawn more than superficial attention from many wedding guests or business travellers, but it has kept dozens if not hundreds of harpists in work, and contributed significantly to the instrument's revival. The harp can even be heard in what used to be its typical setting, in the drawing rooms of stately homes: Powys Castle and Sudeley House are among those that provide harp recitals for the benefit of tourists. Even the folk harp (which was not considered as separate from the "classical" harp until 30 years or so ago) is booming, with small but active clubs keeping alive the Scottish, Welsh and Irish traditions.

The cost of a new harp has always been high because of the degree of craftsmanship required, drawing on mechanical and metalwork skills as well

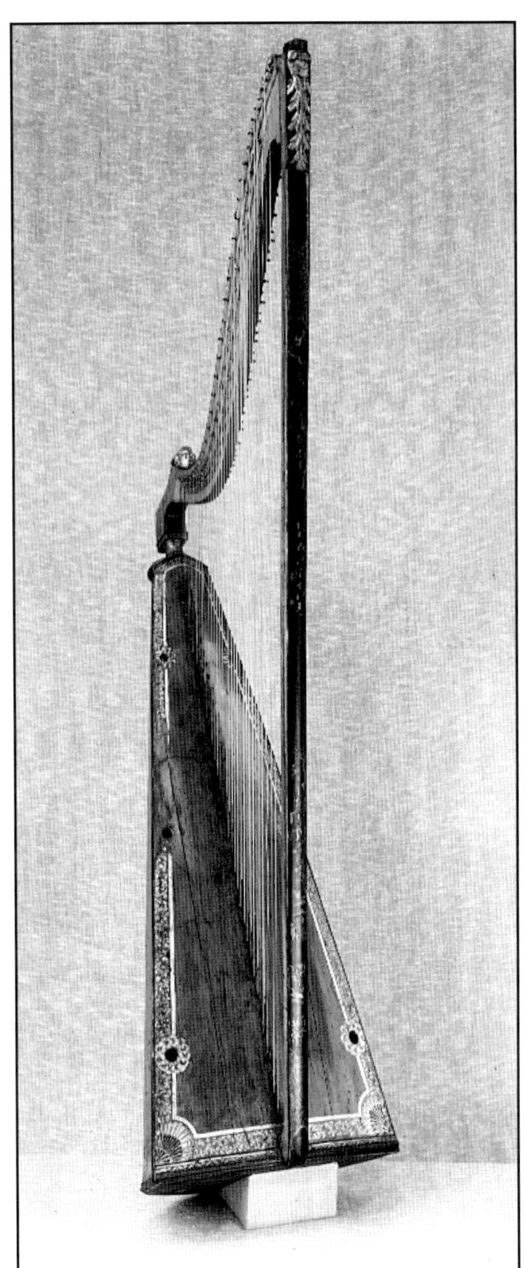

The Welsh harp is still an instrument with a great following, and features regularly in Welsh culture festivals.

as precision woodwork and musical knowledge. In 1820 a new harp cost £80, about the same as a large house in the centre of London; the price of a modern concert instrument – well into five figures rather than two – looks cheap by comparison but still puts off prospective players.

However, Clive Morley is keen to draw in new players, and provides schemes whereby a basic instrument can be rented for a few months to give the parents of a budding harpist chance to decide if it's worth taking the plunge and buying one. He points out that a folk harp costs a few hundred pounds – little more than a reasonable piano, violin or flute, in fact. Hundreds if not thousands of Welsh children take up the harp each year in preparation for the youth Eisteddfod in Wales, where the instrument is still a major part of the country's vigorous cultural life.

The harp will probably always be on the fringe of classical music; the harp world is a small and friendly one, with a handful of performers and just enough music to provide a workable repertoire. In heaven it may survive for all eternity, but for the time being, it's very much alive on earth too.

THE FINEST PERFORMERS

Selected by Harpist David Watkins on the classical side, while harp maker Clive Morley picks out some folk players...

Henriette Renié was an amazing child prodigy and her influence as a composer and teacher was immense. She was one of the first women to be a soloist in her own concerto. She developed poetry, sensibility and virtuosity in her technique, which was pushed to extraordinary limits.

Following her has been Susanne McDonald, now at Indiana State University. She's the top US player and is producing some wonderful younger performers, but doesn't play much now. One of her pupils worth watching out for is Naoko Yoshino, an astonishing Japanese player.

At the end of his career, but still sometimes playing marvellously, is the Basque Nicanor Zabaleta. After the war he was the first harpist jetting round the world and was a real ambassador for the instrument. He was criticised early on for doing too many transcriptions, so he made a tremendous effort to find original harp music.

A well-known name from her TV appearances is the Spaniard Marisa Robles, a very exciting player who has brought the harp to a popular audience. France used to be the home of the harp, and Michelle Nordmann is top rated, a typical French player.

Judy Loman of the Toronto Symphony Orchestra is a very impressive and musical player with a typically American technique, and to round up the variety of national styles I'd like to mention two Russians, Vera Dulova of the Russian Harp School and Tatiana Tower, a fine player with the Leningrad Symphony Orchestra. – *David Watkins*

On the folk side, Derek Bell of the Chieftains has brought folk harp to a wide audience, going back to the simple style, while the Bonnie Shaljean has released some good folk music on CD. Mary O'Hara is a tremendous artist and quite a poet, while Andreas Vollenweider is a good player who does some simple but effective stuff. – *Clive Morley*

THE BEST CD RECORDINGS

Chosen by David Watkins

Mozart's Flute and Harp Concerto – one of the few works by major composers of the period – was written for the Duke de Gignes in 1778; Mozart said his daughter was "magnifique" at playing the harp part. The Zabaleta recording on Deutsche Grammophon is pristine and clear (413 552-2).

A rare harp work by a baroque composer is Handel's Concerto No. 6. It was written for the organ, but a harp version of the original manuscript is in the British Museum. It was intended to be played in the interval of an opera and was written for two Welsh players called Powell. Zabaleta has recorded this piece on DG again (427 206-2).

Debussy's Dances for harp and strings are two contrasting pieces. The first, *Danse sacrée*, is a chaste evocation of a procession to a Greek temple with religious feeling. The second, *Danse profane*, is a sleazy slow waltz, almost like Satie. It's very sensual and very sexual. There are many recordings on CD but the best is by Oppenheimer (RCA RD87173).

Of the twentieth-century pieces one that stands out is Ravel's *Introduction and Allegro*. It's the perfect composition, a mini-harp concerto with everything in it, all in just ten minutes. It's also very varied and very exciting. Again, many recordings on CD including one by Skaila Kanga with the Academy of St Martin in the Fields Chamber Ensemble on Chandos (CHAN8621).

THE PIANO

More of a machine than an instrument

The essential sound of the piano is not a satisfying thing. It doesn't sing like a cello or violin; it doesn't have the rich personality or tone-colour of a brass or woodwind instrument. It rumbles muddily in the bass and rattles drily in the top register. But it has two important abilities: it can produce many concurrent lines – as many notes at one time as the player has fingers, and more if the sustain pedal is used to keep previously struck notes ringing on; and it can make a note as loud or soft as required, according to the force with which the key is struck, and so shape a musical phrase. This makes it the most complete medium for expressing Western musical thought, able to express anything from whistled tunes to large-scale 'symphonic' music.

The piano boom started in the nineteenth century, going hand-in-hand with the new romantic movement in music; but the instrument was no overnight success. The piano was already over a hundred years old by the time Beethoven was writing his last sonatas, around the time when it ousted the harpsichord as the standard keyboard instrument.

Keyboard instruments have been around since the early fifteenth century, when the modern keyboard sequence of 'black and white keys' (though with differing colours) was already established. The crystallisation of all possible tones down into the 12 notes of the scale effectively established the systematic sound of Western music: no notes in the cracks between the keys were possible. This is in stark contrast to, say, Persian and North Indian music, which being string-instrument based, uses a much wider range of notes of varying degrees of sharpness and flatness. But the 12-note system of Western music became firmly fixed by the keyboard that even in vocal music no in-between notes were allowed.

The organ and harpsichord suffered from one great drawback. The simple mechanics meant that the loudness of each note could not be varied, making it impossible to give expression to a phrase; the only way of making a crescendo was simply to play more and more notes at a time. The clavichord – an instrument where each key presses a piece of metal onto a metal string until the key is depressed – was 'touch-sensitive': the loudness of each note was determined by how hard the key was pressed. However, the sound produced was extremely quiet and so was out of the question for concert performances or ensembles.

In 1698 the revolution started. Bartolomeo Cristofori, the keeper of instruments at the Medici Court in Florence, started on a complex new instrument that was to be touch-sensitive like the clavichord, but powerful enough to fill a concert chamber. To achieve this required several engineering hurdles to be overcome. Instead of the plucked-string harpsichord system (loud but not touch-sensitive) or the clavichord's pressed-string system (touch-sensitive but too quiet) Cristofori worked with hammers that struck the strings when a key was pressed. By making the hammer start its upward journey close to the strings, there was a good correlation between the strength of the key-press and the volume. But the hammer had to hit the strings very quickly, otherwise it would damp the string's vibration before falling back. The solution was to make the strings bouncier by making them longer and giving them a much higher tension. Then he had to tackle the problem of a hard key-press making the hammer bounce back up from its rest position to hit the strings a second time: he got round this by an escapement that came into action when the hammer came down, after hitting the string, taking it further down than its resting point, and by adding a check that would stop it bouncing back up. Finally he fitted dampers to stop non-sounded strings resonating. He called it a harpsichord with *piano e forte* – with 'soft and loud' – and the name stuck.

Cristofori's three surviving models, dating from the 1720s, are astonishingly sophisticated. They look and sound like harpsichords, but they behave like modern pianos. The only problem was that, like Charles Babbage's computers of the nineteenth century, they were too far ahead of their time – too complex for anyone else to reproduce and not commercially viable. Cristofori's designs were not really bettered until 150 years later, but at least they stimulated the piano industry. A few makers were inspired to similar work, but with little immediate effect on the musical scene: J S Bach was said to be impressed by two Silbermann pianos owned by Frederick the Great in 1747, but the dominant keyboard instrument was still the harpsichord, and it fell to Bach's sons to develop the piano as a viable instrument.

Over the last decades of the eighteenth century the piano was stimulated from the top down, as composers wrote to exploit the lyrical possibilities of the piano. C P E Bach's music for the clavichord which utilised the touch-sensitivity of the instrument influenced Haydn's piano writing with great impact on the later piano sonata; W F Bach's harpsichord fugues worked so well on the new piano that the style influenced piano writing; and J C Bach gave the first public piano recital in London in 1768. Mozart's piano sonatas and concertos, especially in the slow movements, utilised the developing piano to its fullest effect: his lyrical lines, well-rounded with dynamic markings, would have sounded bare and jerky on the harpsichord, but on the piano they could live and breathe. Phrases should, Mozart said, "flow like oil". The eloquence of the piano stimulated Haydn's later keyboard writing, bringing out his natural wit, humour and feel for colour. Haydn's piano sonatas on a harpsichord would be like a singer heard through a telephone.

However, Haydn and Mozart were writing for quite different instruments. Mozart's Viennese piano was a little box whose rather flimsy case was strengthened by several internal struts; a tough instrument that could be carted around safely. The English piano, one of which Haydn bought years after being thunderstruck by the sound in his London years, was dubbed a "double-bass on its side". The strength came purely from the outer case, which without the damping of any struts could resonate freely. The differences were marked. Vienna was filled with its piano's slightly pingy, clear, cutting notes that sounded immediately on impact; London's drawing rooms and concert chambers resounded to the English piano's lightly damped wash of sound. They came out in the music too: for example, the admonition of Emperor Franz Joseph to Mozart that his music had "too many notes" was not applicable to his Viennese piano writing, which perfectly suited the medium. On the other hand, some of Dussek's music – written for the English piano – is best suited to that instrument, such as his

dance movements where bass lines utilise the resonance for a bagpipe-like drone effect.

But the Viennese piano was a Neanderthal, doomed to extinction because of its rival's flexibility and capacity to adapt. To cater for the ever-larger concert halls, louder meant better, and the stiff Viennese piano couldn't be engineered to be much bigger and therefore louder. The English piano, on the other hand, had the potential to be beefed up: first by a wooden frame, eventually by an iron one. Modern Steinways are the descendants of the English line of pianos.

By 1800 the harpsichord was hanging on through sheer market force: it was the instrument still most likely to be found in front rooms. But composers were writing music for the piano and it was only a matter of time before it took over. Publishers, mindful of appealing to as wide an audience as possible, would put "for harpsichord or piano" on the cover of their music scores – as they did for Beethoven's *Moonlight* Sonata of 1801, a piece that clearly works on the piano and doesn't on the harpsichord. But frontispieces gradually became "for piano or harpsichord", and by the end of Beethoven's life, "for piano". He, after all, was the composer who probably did most to kill off the harpsichord. The volcanic force in his writing, such as in the powerful opening chords of his *Hammerklavier* Sonata, would not have worked on anything but the new modern pianos being developed with a stronger and louder sound than anything before. He was not just following the development of the technology, however: he was profoundly deaf when he wrote most of his later piano works, and the sound of the piano he had heard before losing his hearing was that of the lighter, more genteel early Viennese model. But Beethoven's revolutionary instincts enabled him to write music that exploited new sounds he couldn't hear.

The piano was developing all the time, with various additions and "improvements" being made. Some models from around the Mozart-Beethoven period appear to have been designed for novelty as much as musical value. They had a variety of foot or knee pedals operating mutes and moderators; one piano by Johann Fritz in 1815 cashed in on the craze for "Turkish" music, with pedals that play drums and cymbals. But some important musical improvements went unnoticed, such as Muzio Clementi's patent "harmonic swell". This was the device of extending each string past its anchoring point so a small resonant wash of sound would continue after a key had been played. By damping the extended strings, the device could be turned on and off at will, giving a subtle and controllable reverberation effect that could add great depth to music – as shown by Clementi himself in some of his own works, which were paid the compliment of being the only music on Beethoven's shelves.

Clementi, an Italian-born Englishman who was buried in Westminster Abbey, was one of several great piano craftsmen in the early nineteenth century. Conrad Graf and Anton Walter are the other big names; Walter built Mozart's piano, while Graf could list Beethoven, Chopin and Schumann among his customers, along with Schubert, whose piano was later bought by Brahms. The Graf is considered the king of early pianos, but the company went out of business later in the century, feeling that the metal frames being introduced were unmusical. Meanwhile in England, factory-made Broadwood pianos were being churned out in hundreds.

In the mid nineteenth century, big new pianos with stronger frames, higher tension strings and thus louder sound, were developing hand-in-hand with the big new romantic music. It was the age of the virtuoso, with playing techniques changing as well as the music. The older pianos (which nowadays would be called "fortepianos"), having such a light touch,

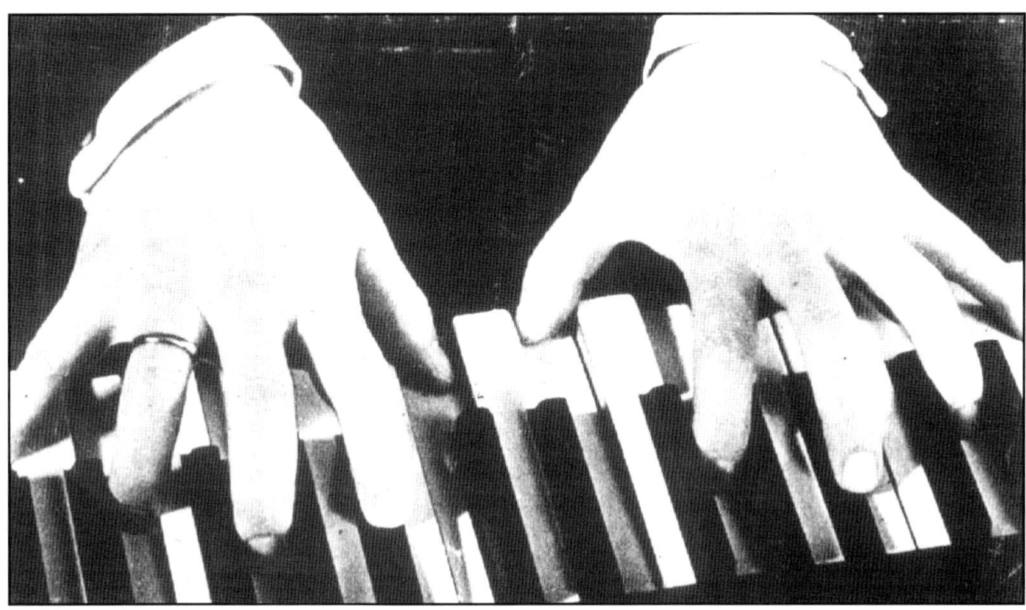

The hands of the composer-pianist **Sergei Rachmaninov** were legendary for their size: he could finger wide-spread chords that few players in the world could manage.

were played with the hands close to the keyboard and moving horizontally rather than vertically. But from about 1850, the new iron-framed pianos with their big splashy sound were being exploited by individuals such as Liszt, whose hands descended from great heights to thump out their astonishing pyrotechnics. John Field, one of the 'old school' who is credited with the development of the Nocturne, was so surprised when he saw a Liszt performance that he is said to have asked "does he bite?".

By the beginning of the twentieth century, when Debussy was establishing impressionism in music with his *Préludes* for piano, factory-made upright pianos were becoming a familiar fixture in the homes made increasingly wealthy by the industrial revolution of the previous decades – with an attendant explosion for the music publishers of piano arrangements of everything. After the depression of the 1930s, however, other forms of entertainment – radio, cinema and eventually television – drove the piano out of the front room. The age of the virtuoso-composer finally died out with Rachmaninov, in 1943, and the piano settled back from its nineteenth-century heyday into being a more mainstream instrument, used for a specific purpose by a composer rather than by default.

The recent interest in authentic music has seen many players such as Melvyn Tan and Malcolm Bilson playing the music of Mozart and others on the instrument the composer knew – usually, modern copies. Though the mechanics of old pianos deteriorate with time, they can be replaced. The wooden cases and frames of good makers on the other hand survive the years very well because the top craftsmen would use very high quality and well-seasoned wood to start with, often over a hundred years old. One Broadwood piano owned by Beethoven – and subsequently, Liszt – was restored in 1992 and played by Tan on an EMI CD of music that Beethoven probably played on the instrument.

As elsewhere in music, there are vociferous pro- and anti-authenticists; some say the elegance and splendour of Mozart's lines are best expressed with the light touch of the Viennese piano rather than the booming modern grand, while others say that the quiet voice of the older piano makes it inaudible in the concert hall – even in Mozart's time there were complaints about balance. At least the effect on mainstream piano playing has been to make all players look back at the Urtext (original) versions of the scores and to be very critical of subsequent "corrections" by editors.

The whole range of piano types can be seen at Finchcocks Museum, near Tonbridge in Kent, which has one of the biggest collections of early keyboard instruments in the world: nearly a hundred, with every big name from Graf to Walter, Clementi to Broadwood well represented. The range of sounds produced by these mostly hand-made, highly individual instruments is astonishing, from the bright immediacy of the Viennese pianos to the rich swell of the English models. Most are still playable, having been carefully restored. Richard Burnett, who runs Finchcocks, has recorded several CDs on the Amon Ra label which demonstrate the sounds of the various pianos in the music of the period.

It's unlikely that we'll see the piano changing much now. The days of models that were designed as elegant pieces of furniture as much as instruments have gone. But it could be argued that the piano is in yet another phase of its development – not, this time, one of mechanical development, but rather a reappraisal of when certain versions of the mechanics are appropriate to the music being played, and when they are not. And that, after all, is what the history of the piano is: not a catalogue of engineering advances, but a constantly developing means of making and defining music.

THE FINEST PERFORMERS

Selected by Roderick Swanston, Principal Lecturer of the Royal College of Music in London

The nineteenth century was the great age of piano virtuosos, and something of their style lived on in the performances of their successors. Among the greatest was Sergei Rachmaninov who, typical of the Russian tradition, combined great pianist and composer in one. His recordings show that his style was surprisingly restrained – almost matter-of-fact, given the way his music is usually treated. Of a slightly later generation but of a quite different temperament was Vladimir Horowitz, probably the last of the great pianistic showmen.

Russia has continued to turn out great piano virtuosos to the present day, boasting such piano giants as Emil Gilels, Vladimir Ashkenazy and in particular Sviatoslav Richter, who has maintained the tradition of pioneering new music. He was spotted early in his career by Prokofiev, who wrote his Ninth Sonata for him.

In central Europe pianists have gravitated towards the Viennese classics, making a point of faithfulness to the musical text. A pioneer of this approach was Artur Schnabel whose attitude seems most obviously carried on today in the thoughtful playing of Alfred Brendel.

No part of the world has had a monopoly in producing great pianists in the recording era. They have come from far afield: Artur Rubinstein from Poland; Claudio Arrau from Chile; and Fou Ts'ong from China, for example. Britain has also had its share of brilliant players: John Ogdon combined a powerful technique with sometimes fearsome musical intellect, qualities also evident in

Glenn Gould, the most engaging and eccentric, player of modern times. His career was tragically cut short by a fatal stroke at the age of 50.

the playing of Barry Douglas. British pianists are also amongst the best champions of unusual repertoire: Margaret Fingerhut for example has championed works by Dukas, Stanford and Bax, while Rolf Hind recorded a magnificent performance of Elliott Carter's daunting Sonata.

As a coda, it's also worth noting that the piano is not just a solo instrument: there have been some great accompanists this century, notably Gerald Moore and Benjamin Britten. The art is now being carried on by the extraordinarily enterprising Graham Johnson.

The Best CD Recordings

Chosen by Roderick Swanston

Being limited to recommending half-a-dozen or so piano CDs is rather like picking the proverbial eight records for a desert island: 80 would be more like it.

My favourite Brahms player was the American pianist, Julius Katchen, whose recording of Brahms's last piano works, Op. 117–19, is among the most sensitive piano-playing I know, (part of a six-disc set: Decca 430 053-2). Quite as good though was his performance of Brahms's first two Piano Trios with Josef Suk and János Starker (Decca 421 152-2).

Choosing a Chopin player is like running through all the players there have ever been. I particularly like Peter Katin playing the Nocturnes on Olympia (OCD 254) and Claudio Arrau's selection on Philips (426 147-2). Katin excels in poetic sensitivity whereas Arrau has a magisterial control of the music.

Late Beethoven presents special challenges to pianists, among them the control of piano tone (those impossible trills!) and the ability to grasp the music as a whole. I especially like Maurizio Pollini's performances of the last five sonatas (Deutsche Grammophon 419 199-2).

Mozart's piano concertos are amongst my favourite works, and I like performances both on period and modern instruments. But one essential disc for me is Clifford Curzon and Benjamin Britten doing the concertos Nos. 20 and 27 (Decca 417 288-2). On every level this is consummate music making by two great artists.

The piano has changed a good deal over the last 200 years, and it's only recently that we have really become sensitive to how much piano music has been affected by the particular sounds and mechanisms of the instruments of the day. I especially value the revelations of Richard Burnett's performances from Finchcock's, particularly his recording of Mozart's Piano Quartets (Amon Ra CD-SAR31) and, for fun, that of Gottschalk's piano music on an Erard of 1886, a marvellous monster of a piano (Amon Ra CD-SAR32).

The pianist I most admire, whose musical and technical versatility excels all others, is Sviatoslav Richter. Hard to know where to begin with recommending one CD by him, but a good idea of his range can be gauged from a wonderful disc with Haydn's Thirty-ninth Sonata, Brahms's Violin Sonata in G and Shostakovich's Violin Sonata (Mezhdunarodnaya Kniga MK418014). The recording is as intense and gripping as his live performances.

ABOUT THIS DISC

We wanted to illustrate the articles in this book in the best way possible – by letting you hear the instruments. So we joined forces with Naxos Records to provide the tracks on the disc that comes with this book: 15 tracks, one for each instrument.

We chose Naxos for several reasons. The first is that, despite being a budget-price label – each disc is a new digital recording but costs just £5 or so, an amazing bargain – most of the recordings they have made have received widespread praise from the established music critics. So, if you hear a track on our disc which you enjoy, you can buy the full-length disc from which the extract is taken for a very small outlay. (We've restricted ourselves to single discs, rather than multi-CD sets, for that reason.)

The choice of which pieces to put on the disc went something like this. First, the order: it seemed reasonable to put instruments into groups (strings, woodwind, brass, etc) and then arrange them roughly top-to-bottom in terms of their range – so we'd start with the violin, viola, cello, bass and so on. That way the contrast between instruments of the same group should show up most clearly when playing the disc. Though the piano is a percussion instrument, strictly, it seemed odd to put it next to the xylophone, so the piano track ends the disc selection.

Then there was the choice of tracks. In each instance we've chosen a whole movement, rather than an extract, which illustrates the sound and character of the instrument, and also sits well on the disc with the tracks before and after it: there is no point having seven fast movements in succession, for example. Wherever possible we've used well-known music.

The descriptions that follow for each track are in three sections. First we describe the circumstances surrounding the composition of the work; then we describe the music itself; then we give details of other music on the disc from which the extract is taken.

So we want this disc to be not only the ideal companion to the articles in the book – and an enjoyable listen in its own right – but also to serve as an introduction to works you may have heard but not be familiar with, and want to buy in their entirety.

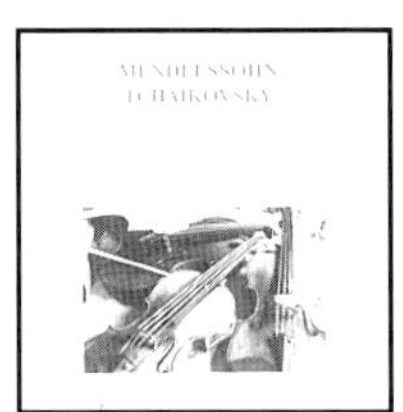

1 TCHAIKOVSKY VIOLIN CONCERTO IN D MAJOR

– finale, Allegro vivacissimo (11:25) from Naxos 8.550153
Takako Nishizaki (violin); Slovak Philharmonic Orchestra/Kenneth Jean

HOW THE MUSIC WAS WRITTEN

The popularity of Pyotr Il'yich Tchaikovsky (1840–1893) with the record-buying and concert-going public, despite often hostile criticism, is probably down to the emotional nature of his music: like many Russians, the moods in his life and his music ran very deep. The Violin Concerto was written in spring 1878 during a trip to Switzerland Tchaikovsky had undertaken to flee his disastrous marriage. It was rejected by the violinist Tchaikovsky offered it to, Leopold Auer, as unplayable, and after its controversial premiere in 1876 it was condemned by several critics – yet it has stayed popular with the public ever since and is now an established masterpiece for the violin.

THE MUSIC

The finale is, like many concerto finales, in sonata-rondo form – that is, a tune is repeated several times with varying episodes in between. The whole movement is full of drive and impetus, and it seems like the orchestra is pushing the soloist on to do ever more daring things.

The whirling figure started by the orchestra is quickly taken up by the violin (0:14) which plays around with the music and even throws in a little pizzicato – plucking the strings with the fingers instead of using the bow (0:32). The orchestra joins in at 1:00 and we hear 'the tune' for the first time. The violin plays little variations on the tune until at 2:15 there's a rather lugubrious little contrasting melody, using the lower range of the violin, which turns into some fast work for the soloist. A slow, reflective passage – but not the deep tragedy Tchaikovsky often wrote – leads up to the reappearance of the rondo tune at 4:30. At 5:30 there's chance for the violin to show off double-stopping (playing two notes at once) and that contrasting melody comes back at 6:05. More showing off for the soloist is followed by a dialogue (up to 7:30) between the woodwinds who exchange the initial phrase played by the violin, as if discussing its merits. The main tune for violin and orchestra comes back at 8:55 and we hurtle towards the big finish.

THE DISC

The Tchaikovsky Concerto is coupled with another of the most established violin concertos: the one by Mendelssohn, written in 1844 – another work full of tunes that shows off the violin superbly.

2 TELEMANN VIOLA CONCERTO IN G MAJOR

– first movement, Largo (3:44) from Naxos 8.550156
Ladislav Kyselak (viola); Capella Istropolitana/Richard Edlinger

HOW THE MUSIC WAS WRITTEN

Georg Philipp Telemann (1681-1767) is often the forgotten man of the baroque era, with names of his contemporaries such as J S Bach, Handel and Vivaldi looming larger in concerts and recordings. Things were different then. When Bach was appointed to a job as Cantor of St Thomas's church in Leipzig, one Dr Platz said reluctantly that they'd had to go for Bach because "the best wasn't available" – the best being Telemann. History, however, has so completely reversed Dr Platz's judgement that Telemann's music is only now beginning to reappear on disc and in the concert hall in the way that it deserves. The Viola Concerto is only one of thousands of pieces that he wrote – he is listed in the *Guinness Book of Records* as the most prolific composer ever.

THE MUSIC

After the pyrotechnics of the violin in the previous track, the graver and more stately low voice of the viola comes as quite a contrast. This *Largo* shows off that contrast very effectively. A graceful, slightly wistful theme in the strings is backed by harpsichord continuo – that is, a harpsichord used to provide a rhythmic support rather than a tune. The viola enters at 0:32, taking up the theme, ideally suited to its low, dark tones. Even when it's playing high up, at 2:30 for example, it couldn't be mistaken for a violin because of the depth to the tone. And when it even gets slightly athletic, at 2:50, it couldn't be mistaken for a violin either, as the violin would be much crisper and brighter.

THE DISC

This extract comes from an all-Telemann disc which in addition to the Viola Concerto features the Recorder Suite in A minor, the Concerto in F major for three violins, and the Concerto for two horns. Ideal music for listening, relaxing to, enjoying a meal with, or doing the ironing by!

3 J S BACH CELLO SUITE NO. 1 IN G MAJOR

– first movement, Prelude (2:27); fifth movement, Menuet I & II (3:19) from Naxos 8.550677
Csaba Onczay (cello)

HOW THE MUSIC WAS WRITTEN

'Bach' means 'stream' in German, and Johann Sebastian Bach (1685–1750) certainly produced a steady stream of music. He was a busy man: as well as over a thousand catalogued works, virtually all masterpieces written mostly in the course of fulfilling his various musical posts, he was married twice, had 20 children, and even managed to get thrown into prison for a few days after wrangles over a contract. These cello pieces were written for a musical colleague in 1717 while Bach was working in Cöthen.

THE MUSIC

All the Six Suites Bach wrote for solo, unaccompanied cello are based on sets of five or so dances, with a Prelude to introduce them. The Prelude usually has an almost improvised feel to it, in contrast with the tighter structures of the dance movements. Although called 'dance movements', with names the same as popular dances of the time, no-one would actually have attempted to dance to them in Bach's day – they were purely music to be played and listened to.

After the mournful voice of the viola, the bigger, bolder and more robust sound of the cello is perfectly demonstrated in these two movements from the First Suite. The Prelude has a driving quality to it, thanks to the G string used as a constant bass note, and it's the resonances of the open strings that give the piece its feeling of size (such as in the climb up to the climax of the Prelude at 2:00 or so, where the bass note is on an open string).

The Prelude is followed here by the fifth movement of the Suite, which consists of two minuets: the first (2:30) is bright, while the contrasting second one (3:45) is sadder, moving to G minor from G major. The brighter first Minuet is repeated at 5:10 to round off the movement.

THE DISC

The first three Suites for Solo Cello (or, if you like to think of Bach's music as it is listed in the standard "Bach Werke Verzeichnis", "Bach Work List", BWV1007, 1008 and 1009) are all on this disc. The other three are on Naxos 8.550678. The prospect of over two hours of solo cello sounds a recipe for boredom, but the variety of mood and invention in these Bach masterpieces makes them, like much of the baroque, ideal music to have in the background or to relax to.

4 SAINT-SAENS CARNIVAL OF THE ANIMALS

– sixth movement, "The Elephant" (1:40) from Naxos 8.550335
Czechoslovak RSO/Ondrej Lenárd

HOW THE MUSIC WAS WRITTEN

Camille Saint-Saëns (1835–1921) was already composing by the age of three (sadly none of these very early works survives) and lived until the age of 86, having written a vast quantity of music and also made a reputation as a performer of great talent – Liszt called him the greatest living organist. *The Carnival of the Animals* was composed as a sort of joke: a "zoological fancy" first performed in a friend's home in 1886. Though he wrote many great serious works, this has probably become his most famous legacy.

THE MUSIC

Few musical subjects suit a bass solo – it isn't an agile instrument and can sound very muddy when it attempts to play a melody. Compare the bright and clear range of sounds the cello can produce, as in the previous track, to the murky depths of this track!

But this is a bass solo that works. The lumbering giant in Saint-Saëns's musical parade is perfectly suggested by the engagingly elephantine bass, and though Saint-Saëns would have been profoundly irritated to see the popularity of what he considered a musical trifle, it's easy to see why *Carnival* has become an audience favourite. Another plus for this track is that it doesn't outstay its welcome – by 1:30 the elephant has already wandered off to browse elsewhere.

THE DISC

The Saint-Saëns is coupled with two other works usually earmarked 'popular with children': Britten's *Young Person's Guide to the Orchestra*, a cleverly written but rather formal piece that introduces a Purcell tune across the various instruments in turn; and Prokofiev's engaging *Peter and the Wolf*, a genuinely popular piece with children of all ages in which different players in the story have their own tunes: Peter's is on the strings, his grandfather's on the bassoon, the duck's on the oboe, and so on.

5 BACH SUITE NO. 2 IN B MINOR

– seventh movement, Badinerie (1.30) from Naxos 8.550244
Capella Istropolitana/Jaroslav Dvorak

HOW THE MUSIC WAS WRITTEN

No-one knows for certain when J S Bach wrote his four Suites for Orchestra (nor if he wrote a fifth – he probably didn't). But it could be that he wrote the Suite No. 2 in Dresden for a famous French flautist of the time, Pierre-Gabriel Buffardin, who was renowned for his ability to play fast passages – this might account for the scintillating flute part in the last movement which we have featured on the disc.

THE MUSIC

From possibly the least agile instrument of the orchestra to the most agile. The flute's ability to play almost faster than it can be listened to is exploited by Bach in this last movement – quite a runaway finish to the Suite No. 2. The sprightly theme on the flute, with brisk running accompaniment from strings and harpsichord continuo, is heard right at the beginning and repeated at 0:15. Variations at 0:30 and 0:52 are followed by the dash home.

Because it can be set to quickfire, witty words, the tune has often been used as the basis of humorous songs, by Flanders and Swann, Richard Stilgoe and others.

THE DISC

The Suite No. 2 is on an all-Bach disc, coupled with the Suite No. 1, the Suite in G minor, the Prelude No. 24 in B minor (from the *48*), the *Siciliano* from the Violin Sonata No. 4 and the *Wachet Auf* Chorale Variation. A very good disc of well-known music to have in any collection, not just for fans of Bach or the baroque.

6 MOZART CLARINET QUINTET IN A MAJOR

– second movement, Larghetto (5:57) from Naxos 8.550390 József Balogh (clarinet); Danubius Quartet

HOW THE MUSIC WAS WRITTEN

If it's the clarinet, it has to be Mozart (1756–1791), probably the most celebrated composer who ever lived. The Clarinet Quintet (which is for a clarinet plus a string quartet) was written in 1789 for his friend and colleague Anton Stadler, a clarinettist who specialised in the lower register of the instrument and was experimenting with an instrument that had an even lower range than usual – the basset clarinet. No basset clarinets survive, so we don't know what they would have been like, but the Quintet works superbly well on the modern clarinet.

THE MUSIC

With the long slow melody on the clarinet and the rocking background of the string quartet at the beginning Mozart effectively contrasts the timbres of the soloist and the group, making a very poignant piece.

The low notes at 1:10 are a reminder of the basset clarinet on which Anton Stadler would have played the first performances; as the movement develops, the strings gradually break out into individual lines, beginning with the violin at 1:20 that responds in its own way to the clarinet. After a very brief clarinet solo at 3:15 the opening theme comes back with that comfortingly rocking accompaniment. The movement ends at 5:57 with a resigned little descent into those very low notes again.

THE DISC

The Quintet comes with the Clarinet Quartet in E flat major K374f (which is for clarinet and string trio) and the single-movement Quintet for clarinet, basset-horn and string trio with the involved catalogue number of KA90(580b). The great clarinet chamber music from Mozart on one disc.

7 MOZART OBOE CONCERTO IN C MAJOR

– first movement, Allegro aperto (7:09) from Naxos 8.550345 Martin Gabriel (oboe); Vienna Mozart Academy/Johannes Wildner

HOW THE MUSIC WAS WRITTEN

Mozart's music for wind instruments was usually written to commission (he could be considered the first freelance composer) and the Oboe Concerto was composed probably in 1777 for an oboist colleague, Ferlendis. It turned up later on in another guise: Mozart, pressed for time on a commission for a flute concerto, simply arranged the Oboe Concerto for flute! Incidentally, the K numbers used to catalogue Mozart works come from the list compiled by a lawyer and musicologist, Ludwig von Köchel.

THE MUSIC

From the smooth, airy sounds of the flute and the mellow sound of the clarinet to the sharper, crisper tones of the oboe: a very different quality of sound thanks to that double reed.

You know just what to expect in the first movement of a concerto of Mozart's period: an orchestral introduction before the solo instrument comes in, a period of dialogue between instrument and orchestra, and a short cadenza – where the instrument plays unaccompanied (in Mozart's day the cadenza would be improvised) – before the orchestra comes in with a brief closing statement.

Which is exactly what happens here. The orchestra gives its introduction and the oboe comes in at 1:02 with a scale and one of those long sustained notes that somehow works so well on the instrument. After a period of development between the oboe and orchestra the orchestra sets up the oboe's cadenza in the usual way with the chord at 6:00. The cadenza involves the lowest and highest notes of the oboe's narrow range, with a few fast runs thrown in, and at 6:40 the orchestra joins in briefly to close the movement.

THE DISC

Three Mozart wind concertos on this disc: for oboe, clarinet and bassoon. These three masterpieces, from arguably the greatest writer for winds ever, really show off what each instrument can do. The Clarinet Concerto in particular is well-known and has been used in many film soundtracks.

8 VIVALDI BASSOON CONCERTO IN E MINOR

– third movement, Allegro (3:00) from Naxos 8.550386
Frantisek Hermann (bassoon); Capella Istropolitana/Jaroslav Krcek

HOW THE MUSIC WAS WRITTEN

Antonio Vivaldi (1678–1741) wrote a lot more than just *The Four Seasons* – there are several hundred concertos known for certain and probably plenty more that have been lost. He spent much of his time teaching music to the girls in the Ospedale della Pietà in Venice; there must have been some formidable musicians among them, because many of the works he wrote for them are of extreme difficulty – the bassoon concertos (he wrote nearly 40 of them) are a case in point.

THE MUSIC

The urgent opening, with its interjections in descending scales, will be familiar in style to anyone who's heard a Vivaldi concerto before. The bassoon comes in at 0:30 sounding very worried and agitated. Those fast passages, such as the one at 1:00, are as hard to play as they sound – obviously the girls at the Pietà had very nimble fingers on their clumsy old-style bassoons!

The familiar baroque set-up of solo instrument backed by strings and harpsichord continuo carries on the rather fretful activity. The sound of repeated jumps from low to higher notes has a very characteristic effect on the bassoon, and Vivaldi exploits it at 2:20 – and the gruff lower register of the instrument at 2:47.

THE DISC

There are seven Vivaldi wind and brass concertos on this disc: three for flute (in F major, *La tempesta di mare*, RV433, in D major, *Il cardellino*, RV428, and in G minor, *La notte*, RV439); two for trumpet (which are actually transcriptions from other works); and one for oboe (in D minor RV454) in addition to this bassoon concerto. Fans of the *Four Seasons* will find plenty more to enjoy on this disc: definitely music to be played loudly on a summer day with the windows open!

9 MOZART HORN CONCERTO NO. 4 IN E FLAT MAJOR

– third movement, Rondo (3:29) from Naxos 8.550148
Milos Stevove (horn); Capella Istropolitana/Josef Kopelman

HOW THE MUSIC WAS WRITTEN

The horn concertos all come from late in Mozart's life – though that only means his late twenties and early thirties – and were written for Joseph Leutgeb, a horn player who became one of Mozart's close friends. (Mozart's father Leopold lent money to Leutgeb to buy a cheese shop in Vienna. Four years later the loan was not yet repaid – a fact which may have endeared Leutgeb even more to Mozart, who had mixed feelings about his father.) Though numbered Four, this was actually the third concerto Mozart wrote, and was completed on 26 June 1786.

THE MUSIC

Probably the most famous movement from Mozart's horn music starts right off with the tune. And as usual, with horn concertos, the final movement is in six-eight (a DA-da-da da-da-da rhythm) recalling the hunting-horn origins of the instrument.

It's a cheerful, robust rondo, with that tune coming back at 1:04, 1:55 and finally 2:53, interspersed with little episodes of other material. The third 'episode' at 2:10 sounds as if it's going to be the same as the first one, but changes shape – Mozart no doubt smiled when he wrote that – and at 2:30 the horn actually does an impression of a hunting-horn, but in a low part of its range – the rough and very earthy result on a horn of Mozart's day would have been intentionally comical. It all goes to form an affectionate musical tribute to and portrait (warts and all) of Leutgeb from his close friend.

THE DISC

All four Mozart horn concertos, plus the Rondo in E flat major, K371, fit nicely onto one CD. Same composer, same dedicatee, same instrument – and yet what a great variety in the music. Irresistible stuff.

10 Vivaldi 'Trumpet Concerto' in B flat Minor

– second movement, Largo (2:22) from Naxos 8.550386 Miroslav Kejmar (trumpet); Capella Istropolitana/Jaroslav Krcek

HOW THE MUSIC WAS WRITTEN

Another of Vivaldi's prolific concerto output, though this one lacks an RV number because it's a transcription of another of his works. (The letters RV come from "Ryoms Verzeichnis" – "Ryom's register", the list of Vivaldi's works compiled by musicologist Paul Ryom.) Vivaldi didn't write trumpet concertos for the girls at the Pietà – it wasn't considered a suitable instrument for a young lady – but these transcriptions, by Jean Thilde, suit the baroque style of trumpet playing very well.

THE MUSIC

After the earthy (and what would have been Mozart's day rough-and-ready) sounds of the horn comes the brightly polished grandeur of the trumpet – though this *Largo* shows a side to the instrument a little different from the fanfares found in much baroque music. This transcription puts the trumpet high up in its range straight away – in Vivaldi's day the trumpet had gaps in its lower range. The piece seems to lose itself (perhaps in reminiscence of some courtly love?) at 0:53, and the trumpet is silenced for a while; but it comes back at 1:31 with its slightly regretful melody, supported as ever by the harpsichord continuo.

THE DISC

See track 8 for details.

11 Mozart Requiem

– Tuba mirum (4:37) from Naxos 8.550235 Magdaléna Hajóssyová (soprano); Jaroslava Horská (alto); Jozef Kundlák (tenor); Peter Mikulás (bass); Slovak Philharmonic Chorus and Orchestra/Zdenek Kosler

HOW THE MUSIC WAS WRITTEN

It's one of the most moving stories in music: Mozart, on his death bed at just 35, dictating the Requiem that he'd had commissioned from him, knowing that it would turn out to be a Requiem for his own death. Contrary to anything suggested by the film *Amadeus*, his rival Salieri wasn't there; just relatives and some of his pupils, who were trying to write down the notes he was dictating. He didn't get very far – his last words were in fact an attempt to dictate a drum part to the *Lacrimosa*. At five to one on the morning of 5 Dec 1791, he died.

THE MUSIC

This is probably the most famous use of the trombone in all music – which is why, although a Requiem is obviously a vocal piece, it's on this disc. The difference in timbre between the bright trumpet of the previous track and the subdued trombone of this one is obvious.

The solo trombone call that opens this movement, the fourth of Mozart's Requiem, is the sound of the Last Trump – the summoning of the world to Judgement Day. The bass, imitating the call, sings "Tuba mirum spargens sonum" – translation can cause confusion, as 'tuba' is translated 'trumpet', and in fact we have a trombone playing. At 0:38 he repeats the words ("The trumpet makes its awesome sound" might be a translation) and his voice weaves in and out of the trombone's intricate line up to 1:20.

As the movement continues, the bass is replaced by the tenor, who gives way to the alto, who is in turn replaced by the soprano, and they then sing together how all mankind will be judged.

THE DISC

This disc of Mozart's Requiem provides the 'standard' completion of the work Mozart left incomplete by his pupil Süssmayr. There's no coupling because the work lasts over 50 minutes – but it would be a strange person who would want to put on anything else after Mozart's profoundly moving farewell to the world.

12 SAINT-SAENS CARNIVAL OF THE ANIMALS

– thirteenth movement, "Fossils" (1:40) from Naxos 8.550335
Czechoslovak RSO/Ondrej Lenárd

HOW THE MUSIC WAS WRITTEN

The second track on our disc, after track 4, from Saint-Saëns's "zoological fancy" from 1886. He used the term 'animals' loosely: as well as elephants, kangaroos, fish in a very watery-sounding aquarium, hens and the rest, there are those strange animals called 'pianists' (who play scales very badly) and this track, "Fossils". The original orchestration for his little joke was much smaller than the full-size we're used to today: two pianos, two violins, viola, cello, double bass, flute, clarinet, mouth organ and xylophone.

THE MUSIC

Another short piece, just 1:30, about which there's not much to say – this is not academic music to be dissected like a fossil. And therein lies the joke: the brittle sound of the xylophone is just right for suggesting fossilised bones in a light-hearted way, audible clearly even when the rest of the orchestra is playing.

This piece is familiar to British television audiences as it was used to accompany a series of commercials for a supermarket.

THE DISC

See track 4 for details.

13 HANDEL SUITE NO. 1 IN A MAJOR

– fourth movement, Gigue (1:42) from Naxos 8.550415
Alan Cuckston (harpsichord)

HOW THE MUSIC WAS WRITTEN

Georg Frideric Handel (1685–1759) was born in the same year as Bach just a few dozen miles away, yet the two never met. Handel moved to London, settling there and producing some of his greatest oratorios and operas – always box-office hits – and plenty of instrumental music. These harpsichord suites were from a collection published in 1720 but using material stretching back to his teenage years. Of course, part of the rationale for publishing them was for the public to play, but he had another more commercial reason – namely, that a pirate edition of his harpsichord music had just come out in Amsterdam!

THE MUSIC

A Gigue – as its name implies – was based on a dance, though you'd have had to be a lively mover to dance to one as rapid as this. Three feet might have come in handy too, as it moves in triple time. It was a common element of instrumental dance suites around Handel's time, and provides a very colourful ending to his first suite.

But then fast-running music suits the harpsichord much better than slow music, because of the quick decay of a harpsichord note. The piercing clarity of the instrument is used to full effect in this piece: though several fairly fast lines are going on at once, the ear can easily hear them separately.

A line imitating the opening phrase is brought in on top of it at 0:05, and again at 0:10, but each time starting on a different note of the scale, as if the music is chasing itself up the keyboard – as in the name 'fugue', meaning 'flight'. The lines all manage to catch up with each other at 0:50 and the process starts again.

THE DISC

Alan Cuckston plays five Handel suites on this disc: No. 1 in A major, No. 2 in F major, No. 3 in D minor, No. 4 in E minor, and No. 5 in E major.

14 MOZART CONCERTO IN C MAJOR FOR FLUTE AND HARP

– first movement, Allegro (9:57) from Naxos 8.550159
Jiri Valek (flute); Hana Müllerova (harp); Capella Istropolitana/Richard Edlinger

HOW THE MUSIC WAS WRITTEN

Mozart loved wind instruments – except for the flute, which legend says he hated writing for as much as the harp. So why did he combine them in this 1778 work? It could well be that, faced with the prospect of a commission for a flute concerto and a harp concerto, he lumped them together to cut down the effort. Alas, it seems he never got paid for the result, and he didn't even get any benefits in kind in the form of a teaching job for the Duc de Guines, the flautist who requested the work, and his daughter, the harpist.

THE MUSIC

You would never guess Mozart's distaste for the flute from the music he wrote for it; his similar feelings about the harp are less well hidden. He never wrote another note for the instrument – perhaps surprisingly, considering its popularity at the time – and the writing for the harp here is more like a piano than a harp (such as at 5:20), making it awkward to play.

Yet the piece has remained a firm favourite with audiences. Why? Perhaps it's the relatively straightforward nature of the piece: the commission was for light, pleasant music that was posed no challenges to the listener, and that's exactly what Mozart wrote.

The format is the standard one for a concerto of the time: a longish orchestral introduction (up to 1:29) after which the soloists come in together echoing the orchestra's theme. The flute plays over cascades from the harp as the music develops in an unthreatening way, and the cadenza for the flute and harp comes in on schedule at 8:25. A glissando from the harp at 9:20 beckons the orchestra back to wind the movement up.

THE DISC

The Flute and Harp Concerto is paired with the *Sinfonia concertante* in E flat major, K297b. Both are examples of classical music (in the sense of the classical period rather than classical music generally) at its best.

15 CHOPIN NOCTURNE IN E FLAT MAJOR, OP. 9 NO. 2

(4:29) from Naxos 8.550356
Idil Biret (piano)

HOW THE MUSIC WAS WRITTEN

Frederic Chopin (1810–1849) did not invent the Nocturne – the Irish pianist John Field usually gets the credit for that for his Nocturnes of 1814–35 – but Chopin certainly cornered the market in the genre and will always be associated with them. The three Nocturnes that were published as his Opus 9, of which this is the second, appeared in print in Paris in 1833 dedicated to the pianist wife of the famous piano maker Pleyel.

THE MUSIC

For many people, the piano means Chopin; Chopin means Nocturnes; and Nocturnes means this particular piece. It's so familiar it hardly seems worth describing in detail – and besides, it's the sort of music that is better listened to and enjoyed, than examined to see how it works.

We can only wonder what Chopin would have thought of on hearing his pieces played on a modern piano, with its grander and less intimate sound than the model he'd be used to; but comparing even a modern piano to the sound of the harpsichord in track 13, perhaps it's understandable why the piano so quickly killed it off.

THE DISC

Idil Biret has quickly established herself as a Chopin player of world class thanks to her CD series of the complete solo Chopin piano works. Volume 1, from which this is taken, is a collection of the better-known Nocturnes: Op. 9 Nos. 1 and 2; Op. 9 No. 3; Op. 15 Nos. 1–3; Op. 27 Nos. 1 and 2; Op. 32 Nos. 1 and 2; and two lesser-known ones in C minor and C sharp minor. Any of the series is well worth investigating.

Page	Credit
15,17,35,39, 64, 73, 77,92	Mary Evans Picture Library
18	Christies Colour Library
26,28,52,101,109	Hulton-Deutsch
29	Elgar Foundation
37	Ron Prentice
40-41	Flutemaker's Guild Ltd
48	Rex Features
51	Kobal Collection
54	Ace Photo Agency
55	Photo and modern reeds by Graham Salter, Baroque reeds by Paul Goodwin
71,89	Clive Barda/PAL
78	E T Archive
82,98	Bridgeman Art Library
84-85	Hutchison Library
90	Andrew Garlick
104	Victoria and Albert Picture Library